You're Not Watching Me, Mummy

AND

Try a Little Tenderness

JOHN OSBORNE

You're Not Watching Me, Mummy

AND

Try a Little Tenderness

TWO PLAYS FOR TELEVISION

FABER AND FABER
London & Boston

First published in 1978
by Faber and Faber Limited
3 Queen Square London WC1N 3AU
Printed in Great Britain by
Latimer Trend & Company Ltd Plymouth
All rights reserved

Prior permission must be obtained from the
copyright owner Campbell Connelly & Co. Ltd.,
London, for the inclusion of the song 'Try a Little
Tenderness' in public performances of the play

All applications for professional or amateur
performing rights should be addressed to Robin
Dalton, Robin Dalton Associates, 18 Elm Tree Road, NW8

British Library Cataloguing in Publication Data

Osborne, John, b. 1929
You're not watching me, Mummy; and, Try a
little tenderness.
I. Title. II. Osborne, John, b. 1929. Try a little
tenderness
822'.9'14   PR6029.S39Y/

ISBN 0-571-11240-4

You're Not Watching Me, Mummy

CAST

JEMIMA
LESLIE
MRS COLBOURNE
ROGER
SUSAN
LENA
RONALD
FREDDIE
ANTHONY
KLOB
AUBREY
GIRL
RENÉ
STAGE MANAGER

1. EXTERIOR. NIGHT. SHAFTESBURY AVENUE

Lines of huge coaches are parked outside the theatres waiting for the customers to come out. Hundreds of tourists of all nations pour up and down the street in their shirtsleeves, dripping with cameras, eating hot dogs, staring into the amusement arcades, coming out of Wimpy Bars. And so on. Germans, Japanese, Americans, the moving garbage of modern tourism. During this glimpse of what was once known as 'Up West', there is a smug-sounding voice intoning:

VOICE: *(Off)* And, so, in these days of chronic, rising inflation, we must do all we can to encourage and promote, promote and encourage, I say, the burgeoning British tourist industry. In these days of chronic and steadily rising, rising inflation, we cannot sit back and say calmly 'we are an island'. We are no longer an island. To coin a phrase, no man is an island. And why? Because he can no longer afford it. And we, none of us, can afford it. There was a time, not so very long ago, when you'd say, with justifiable pride, 'I am a Londoner'. Well, today, every visitor to these shores, may say also 'I, too, am a Londoner'. And why? Because he is supporting the very life blood of our economy. That's what counts in these harsh times, *what it brings in to your pocket*. Even if, at times, one feels as if one has lost a little of the old intimacy and—seclusion even. Those days are past and won't return. . . .

2. EXTERIOR. NIGHT. SHAFTESBURY AVENUE

The first theatregoers trickle out on to the pavements, some looking for taxis, waving their programmes.

3. EXTERIOR. NIGHT. SOHO STREET
Against the red sign STAGE DOOR, *a small group of autograph hunters wait quietly.*

4. INTERIOR. NIGHT. STAGE DOOR-KEEPER'S BOX
Looking up from his television set, the stage door-keeper consults his watch. There is a crackling sound from the Tannoy, a silence, and then the sound of applause. He sighs and goes back to his viewing.

5. INTERIOR. NIGHT. THEATRE EXIT DOORS
A clatter of iron bars as a couple crash out into the street, quivering with long-suppressed mirth. The man exclaims, 'Oh, my Gawd! What about *it!' His companion shrieks, 'What about* her!' '*Evening*—Evening Standard *Drama Award! Drama!' They disappear into the street, giggling.*

6. EXTERIOR. NIGHT. SHAFTESBURY AVENUE
The audiences are beginning to come out in force. Chauffeurs open car doors for their owners.

CHAUFFEUR: Enjoy it, madam?

LADY: (*Getting in car*) She's superb. Absolutely superb.

VOICE: (*Off*) And let us make no apologies. We have an enormous treasure house of history, tradition, pageantry, art and culture to offer the world. Architecture, our royal palaces and stately homes and gardens. Shakespeare, Opera, Ballet, Sport and the finest theatre in the world.

7. INTERIOR. NIGHT. STAGE PROMPT CORNER. APPLAUSE
STAGE MANAGER: Oh, *someone's* in a hurry to get home! All right, give the silly buggers another one. (*He presses the tabs switch and the curtain goes up again, with a few sidelong scowls from the line-up of actors.*) Well, Cadburys made a fortune even if the bars didn't. Look at that shower—they think they've had a Cultural Experience—culture!

8. INTERIOR. NIGHT. THEATRE AUDITORIUM

The line-up of the cast. In the middle, the leading man, AUBREY, *and the leading lady,* JEMIMA, *smile at each other, hold hands and step out and bow to the applause.*

9. INTERIOR. NIGHT. THEATRE STALLS

CU audience.

10. INTERIOR. NIGHT. THEATRE STAGE

AUBREY *and* JEMIMA *bowing.*

AUBREY: (*Smiling at audience. Lips not moving*) Good*night*! Silly, tasteless bastards. Come *on*, I want my grub. Bastards. (*Smiling more than ever.*) Crass Nips, Krauts and Yankees! Give us your money and piss off 'ome!
(AUBREY *waves. Curtain falls.*)

11. INTERIOR. NIGHT. STAGE

The actors trail off to the prompt corner.

JEMIMA: If you feel that much contempt, I don't know why you bother.

AUBREY: I need the bread, mate. And my stomach's rumbling.

JEMIMA: I heard it all through the last act. So did the audience I expect.

AUBREY: Best thing they heard tonight.

JEMIMA: Listen, they're not *all* fools, you know.

AUBREY: No?

JEMIMA: I should lay off the grub a bit too. Your paunch is quite repellent in that jacket.

AUBREY: At least I've got something to snuggle up to. All those boring diets of yours.

JEMIMA: You're an actor. Or supposed to be. Try and remember it. Besides, it's disloyal to the audience.
(*They proceed to the corner on their way to the dressing-room.*)

AUBREY: Disloyal! To *them*! Vultures. (*To* STAGE MANAGER.) Milking it weren't you? No late night cruising then?

STAGE MANAGER: Don't you believe it.

AUBREY: Good hunting! Don't get beaten up again if you can.

Jemima won't love you.

JEMIMA: Of course I will. (*Kisses* STAGE MANAGER.) Always.

AUBREY: Still on the dinge kick?

(STAGE MANAGER *nods*.)

What's this one—not our director's driver?

STAGE MANAGER: Oh, he's stale news. He's a boxer.

AUBREY: Heavyweight?

STAGE MANAGER: *And hung.*

AUBREY: Better rehearse your Aircraftsman Ross limp. 'Night.

STAGE MANAGER: 'Night. Don't forget—

JEMIMA: Matinée tomorrow! Will you tell that boring stagehand
not to watch me in my first change? I've got no knickers on.
(*To* AUBREY.) Anyway you've a duty to the author.

AUBREY: Sorry, love, but ladies can't write plays.

JEMIMA: Then why be in them? I know—for the loot.

AUBREY: Just because she fancies you.

JEMIMA: Balls.

AUBREY: Well, she's in your bleeding dressing-room nearly every
night. And laughing at her own lines at the back. Do you
know what they call her?—Eve.

JEMIMA: Eve?

AUBREY: Eve Harrington. You know. All About Eve. She even
imitates your mannerisms, poor old soul. Speech, everything.

JEMIMA: Rubbish.

AUBREY: Afraid she doesn't have your style for it.

JEMIMA: How's the crumpet stakes?

AUBREY: Oh, living off the land.

JEMIMA: Some teenage scrubber, I suppose.

AUBREY: Someone who likes me, paunch and all.

(AUBREY *and* JEMIMA *approach the pass door. He opens it for
her, and she passes through.*)

'Night, love.

JEMIMA: 'Night. Try not to be too sated for the matinée. You
remember, Thursday.

AUBREY: Not much. Give my love to Eve.

JEMIMA: Bitch! Don't get her in the club again.

AUBREY: She wants to be the mother of my child.

JEMIMA: Blimey, she *must* be a little cretin. All *she'll* get is chronic crabs again. 'Night, Aubrey.

AUBREY: 'Night . . .

(JEMIMA *rushes up the corridor to her dressing-room. It is marked No 1, and opens as she approaches. Her dresser,* LESLIE, *is waiting for her.*)

LESLIE: They'll be here in a minute. What's the two extra calls for?

JEMIMA: God knows. Really *thick* house, thick, thick, thick. Keep them out for five minutes. Here—

12. INTERIOR. NIGHT. DRESSING-ROOM

Clutter of clothes, bottles, fridge, souvenirs, wig blocks, dozens of first-night telegrams on the walls, toy animals. The usual. LESLIE *deftly helps* JEMIMA *out of her dress and into her dressing-gown.*

JEMIMA: Oh God, she still hasn't fixed that bloody lining yet! *Look* at it!

LESLIE: I'll take it up to wardrobe—if she hasn't gone home yet.

JEMIMA: Gone!

LESLIE: She has to get her bus to Balham.

JEMIMA: Someone should write a play called 'Last Bus to Balham'. It's what this business is all about nowadays. I *must* have it when I get in.

LESLIE: Will do.

JEMIMA: Got my drink?

LESLIE: On your table. Just opened.

(LESLIE *hangs up* JEMIMA's *dress carefully, and* JEMIMA *flops on to her chair. She stares at herself in the mirror.*)

13. INTERIOR. NIGHT. DRESSING-ROOM

JEMIMA's *reflection in the mirror.*

JEMIMA: Shit! (*She gulps at her glass of champagne, then, placing a ribbon round her hair, proceeds to put cream on her face and remove her make-up. She stops and stares intently at her image, frontal and profile. Pause.*)

(LESLIE *waits.*)

Do you think I need it yet?

LESLIE: What?

JEMIMA: The job—you know—*here*. (*She scrunches up her eyes, wrinkles her nose and wiggles her mouth.*)

LESLIE: 'Course not. I keep telling you.

JEMIMA: But you see me all the time. What do they really think when they all come trooping in here—with a greasy face and an old scarf round my head? I look like the Queen when her horse has lost the Gold Cup. Christ, look at my eyelids! They'll be the first to go.

LESLIE: Laugh lines.

JEMIMA: Balls.

LESLIE: Frown lines.

JEMIMA: Middle bloody age more like. Still, I look better than Harriet and she's two years older. Do you know she always manages to get herself in the papers as thirty-eight? Thirty-eight! If she's thirty-eight, I'm Twiggy. My mother knew her mother in Nairobi and she met a girl who went to school with her well before the war and she swears she's at least forty-seven.

LESLIE: Must be.

JEMIMA: I think it's showing too. Do you know she's not got her date of birth in *Who's Who*? That's not just *common*, it's stupid. People *always* add on ten years. Mine's there forever, I'm afraid. Born Nairobi, December 1932. Geoffrey says she's just had a whole face job only, typically, she went and got a cheap one. And it's a disaster. He said he went to see her the other night and she looked like Minnie Mouse, doesn't move her face.

LESLIE: Daft.

JEMIMA: Sometimes I wish I'd let Paramount bully me into that nose job after all.

LESLIE: Lose that—

JEMIMA: I know, and I lose my unique stage presence and a decent nose. Like Jean, she's got a super nose. Doesn't matter she's such a hopeless actress. (*Pause*) What about my tits?

LESLIE: Lovely—if that's what the men like.

JEMIMA: To hell with the men! What about *these*! (*She hoists her*

16

breasts up for examination. They stare at them.)

LESLIE: No use asking *me* really, is it?

JEMIMA: What about my arse then?

LESLIE: You'd better get off it quick, that's all. They'll all be here in a minute.

JEMIMA: Damn! Why can't they wait! Do you know who was in?

LESLIE: Lena.

JEMIMA: Did you hear her laugh?

LESLIE: You can't help it.

JEMIMA: I never hear it.

LESLIE: Getting deaf in your middle age. You need an ear, nose and throat, not a face job.

JEMIMA: Oh, why do they have to come in for a *second* performance.

LESLIE: You wouldn't like it if nobody came round, now would you?

JEMIMA: Yes, but these lunatics! You used to be so good at protecting me, Les. But that woman about deaf dogs! And that idiotic American who was so rude and stayed all night.

LESLIE: What about *her*—the wife!

JEMIMA: (*Laughing*) God! Mrs Hot Flushes from Philadelphia. Home Maker Extraordinary and Patron of the Arts. (*American accent.*) Arnold and I just *love* your British Theatre! We come *every* summer. We go to Stratford, of course, and now your new National Theatre—

LESLIE: Colditz-on-Thames.

JEMIMA: Arnold is writing a PhD thesis on your new-style theatre and wonders if you would—

LESLIE: Write it for him.

JEMIMA: Hand me that cotton wool, would you, darling?

LESLIE: How was Sir Aubrey tonight?

JEMIMA: Thinking about his belly and his dolly, as usual. I don't understand that attitude, I really don't.

LESLIE: He likes to have a good time, I suppose.

JEMIMA: He's not entitled to a good time. He's in the theatre. Wish he'd do something about that paunch. I told him about it again tonight.

LESLIE: So did I!

JEMIMA: What did he say?

LESLIE: 'Shut up, you old Jessie.' *We* don't have to be young and beautiful like you lot, forever watching your hairline and waistline before you troll around the jungle bunnies in Notting Hill!

JEMIMA: Arrogance of them! They wouldn't like it if their women didn't bother . . . God, actors spend their lives putting on clothes and taking them off. All I seem to do is spend half the day stripping up and down. Oh, I'm so *late* . . . I hope they don't stay for hours like last night. I thought that hag with the teeth from Leicester who said she was at RADA with me would never go.

LESLIE: Was she?

JEMIMA: If she was I don't know how she got past the door the size of her. *I* don't remember her.

LESLIE: B.O., my dear!

JEMIMA: Don't! Mingled with Miss Dior.

LESLIE: D.O.

JEMIMA: Why, *why* do they come round? Just sitting there, as if they expected something to really happen in *here* after you've knocked your arse off for two and a half hours. Staring, saying nothing, waiting, helpless, the world seems to be full of them. We slosh our blood all over the stage for them and what do they do? Sit and wait for a drink!

LESLIE: Paid for out of *your* hard-earned money. I tell you, you shouldn't do it.

JEMIMA: 'Silly to herself.'

LESLIE: Silly to herself she is. Why don't you let me lock it away like you said you would?

JEMIMA: It's just that I can't bear the silence and their shifting. *I* need it, anyway, to unwind. They've got *nothing* to unwind. Just what life is like: with a husband and three point seven kids in Kingston on Thames; and how 'George doesn't really like the theatre and so they never go and, besides they're so busy what with the children, the garden, the car and his mother. Still, they quite liked the show, what are

18

you doing next? Oh, is it on television? Is it ITV or BBC? George only watches BBC and then it's mostly for the sport not *plays*; oh you'd find it ever so good! I expect you must get tired night after night, doesn't it get boring saying the same thing night after night, did you think we were a good audience? Oh, I'm sorry. *We* thought we were rather good. George laughed so much at your bit with the suitcase he knocked my box of chocolates into the stalls. It was awful! It was such a huge box. Well, you might as well make an occasion of it. We must go now'—(after an hour and a half) —'we must catch our train or the baby sitter will disappear. You haven't changed much. How's your mother? Do you see her often? We read your husband had remarried. Oh divorced again is he! Well, we only get the *Daily Telegraph*.' The place *teems* with them, winging their way from Waterloo and Victoria and Charing Cross and all, all of them, every lumpen couple winging their stolid way to *my dressing-room*!

LESLIE: Better get your skates on.

JEMIMA: Oh, *and* a matinée tomorrow. I'll bet some second cousin I've never heard of will turn up with her husband-in-computers.

LESLIE: Why don't you let me say you're not well? You did have your bad back again.

JEMIMA: It's *agony*. Do you think you could walk on my back?

LESLIE: Is there time?

JEMIMA: Let them wait!

(JEMIMA *lies down on her front and* LESLIE *walks slowly up her spine in his socks.*)

14. INTERIOR. NIGHT. DRESSING-ROOM

LESLIE *is making his way by foot up* JEMIMA'S *back.*

JEMIMA: Oh! Oh!

LESLIE: Come on! That doesn't hurt!

JEMIMA: Yes it does. Divine! Oh! There? There! That's it! That's—oh—*it*! You've *got* it. Oh, darling, you're a genius! You got it!

19

(LESLIE *continues to move like a tightrope walker up* JEMIMA's *spine. Pause. She sighs and breathes deeply.*)

I'm very fond of Aubrey but he is pretty pathetic. Men who talk about it never really *do* it much.

LESLIE: I've heard that before.

JEMIMA: You're different. And I wish he'd use some more underarm odour juice.

LESLIE: I hinted to him. He put on something like paint-stripper tonight. Nearly brought the hair off his armpits.

JEMIMA: You wouldn't know it. He just sweats too much. I hate men who sweat.

LESLIE: Can't help it.

JEMIMA: Yes. You can, anyone can help it at his age. Like you can't have armpit mist after you're forty. Oh! Just vanity. Oh! No—go *on*!

LESLIE: Sure?

JEMIMA: Sure. Now do my neck. It feels like rock crystals all round the bottom here . . .

(JEMIMA *sits up on the floor and* LESLIE *massages her neck.*)
Bliss. God, it's better than sex!

LESLIE: *You* think anything's better than sex.

JEMIMA: What do you mean?

LESLIE: Oh, matinées, rehearsals, broadcasts, television—

JEMIMA: I don't.

LESLIE: Doesn't seem time for much else.

JEMIMA: That's not fair.

LESLIE: Including sex.

(JEMIMA *evidently decides to ignore this.*)

JEMIMA: Leslie, did you know what they're supposed to call Lena?

LESLIE: What? Eve, you mean?

JEMIMA: Then it *is* true. I think that's rather unkind of everyone.

LESLIE: Oh, she asks for it. Everyone sends her up. Didn't you know? She even tries to dress like you. That'd take some doing!

JEMIMA: Aubrey says she fancies me. Do you think it's true?

LESLIE: Of course. She can't take her eyes off you.

20

JEMIMA: You mean sexually too?

LESLIE: Oh, I don't know about that. She doesn't go much on men, certainly. But then so many women don't nowadays. Leaves the field a bit more open for *us* or should do—except I suppose it doesn't really.

JEMIMA: I'd no idea. Poor Lena.

LESLIE: She's all right. And you're making her a tidy few bob out of her play.

JEMIMA: It's the play not me.

LESLIE: Don't you believe it. It's the acting that counts—not the writing.

JEMIMA: I think she's very talented. Don't you?

LESLIE: Don't ask me. I just get the feeling—

JEMIMA: What feeling? Ouch! Give me one last go on my back before they start banging the door down. (*She resumes her prone position.*) Well.

LESLIE: Oh, I don't know. I just get the feeling, watching her, with you like, that what she puts down on paper just comes out straight from something she's heard or seen.

JEMIMA: How do you mean?

LESLIE: No garnish, no flavour of her own, do you see what I mean? She just takes it straight from the horse's mouth, from life, no, no *process* in between in *her* and she thinks it will mean something on its own.

JEMIMA: I think you're talking balls.

LESLIE: Yes, me lady.

JEMIMA: It's because she's a woman that's all.

LESLIE: Shouldn't have asked me then.

JEMIMA: I still think she's got talent and it *is* a good play.

LESLIE: It's all right.

JEMIMA: All right? It did win the *Evening Standard* Award for the Best Play.

LESLIE: Big deal. We all know what safe, middlebrow fudge they give that to! Come on, darling.

JEMIMA: I still say it's a good play. Not great but *good*.

LESLIE: Well, the critics think it's intellectual and the audience think it's entertainment, so that's all that matters, isn't it?

JEMIMA: I'm disappointed in you, Leslie. I didn't know you could be so disloyal.

LESLIE: Why should I be loyal to Lena? Have you ever noticed how she treats me?

JEMIMA: No.

LESLIE: Never looks at me, never says 'good evening, how's-your-father' or anything. 'Pour me another glass of white wine, Leslie.' 'Run round and get me a packet of cigarettes, Leslie.' 'Send Jemima some red roses for me will you, Leslie.' 'See if they've towed away my car, Leslie.'

JEMIMA: I didn't know you minded. I wouldn't. Not if she were someone else. I think you all pick on her, that's all. Did you say she was in again tonight?

LESLIE: I *told* you. Honking like a duck with a slow hernia at her own jokes.

JEMIMA: Are you *that* bored with it?

LESLIE: My dear, I'm like a zombie for three hours in this theatre every night. If it weren't for you I wouldn't stick it for a minute.

JEMIMA: So you *are* loyal.

LESLIE: Man's best friend, dear. All my friends say you're the only thing that makes them stay or come and see it in the first place.

JEMIMA: Oh, *come*—it's not that bad. I won't have it . . .

LESLIE: You asked me my opinion. My friends may be just a pack of old queens but some of them do have quite good taste, believe it or not. We're not *all* hidebound.

JEMIMA: What do you mean?

LESLIE: Well, compare this little bon-bon with a bow on it with your last play, darling. It's not in the same league.

JEMIMA: Yes. And it got the worst press of anything I've ever been in.

LESLIE: There you are!

JEMIMA: The audience booed and walked out every night.

LESLIE: Rubbish! Rubbish! I used to listen to them every night.

JEMIMA: You didn't have to stand on the stage and listen to it. Neither did the author.

22

LESLIE: I liked him. He was honest and it showed in his work.
And it was sieved through himself, like a—lifetime's
pondering.

JEMIMA: Lifetime's what? Pondering? Get you!

LESLIE: Not like Eve, anyway. Hers is all posture. She doesn't
even know *what* she feels if you ask me. And if you ask
me—

JEMIMA: I'm not. Let me get up.

LESLIE: No . . . Eve is not what I would call a very honest sort of
person.

JEMIMA: Shut up, you great faggot! That's enough. You're
hurting!

LESLIE: Are you going to New York with it?

JEMIMA: I don't know. Ow! Help!

LESLIE: Don't.

JEMIMA: Ow! Stop it, Leslie. You're hurting!

LESLIE: Because you won't get me coming with you. And you
know you can't live without me getting you in and out of
your tit bag.

JEMIMA: That's enough, I tell you. I've had enough!
(*She yells and the door opens. A young woman in her early
thirties appears. She looks perpetually eager, as if she were
embarking on a confidential questionnaire. She looks surprised
at the spectacle of* LESLIE *standing on top of* JEMIMA'S *back but
it doesn't diminish her wistful smile.* JEMIMA *howls louder than
ever.*)

LENA: Oh—sorry.

JEMIMA: Get off, you sadistic bastard!

LESLIE: There!
(LESLIE *gives a last heavy burst of pressure on* JEMIMA'S *back
and skips lightly off.*)

JEMIMA: I suppose that's what you get those truck drivers to do
to you.

LESLIE: (*Helping* JEMIMA *to her feet*) That, among other things.
(*To* LENA.) Good evening, miss.
(LENA *ignores this.*)

LENA: Are you all right?

JEMIMA: Leslie being a big clumsy nelly, that's all. (*She sits down at her dressing-table.*) Come in and sit down.

LENA: May I?

JEMIMA: Of course. Have a drink.

LENA: I'm not interrupting?

JEMIMA: I'm quite safe with Leslie if that's what you mean. If I was the last woman on earth.

LESLIE: What will you have, miss?

LENA: (*Not looking at* LESLIE) Dry white wine.

LESLIE: Certainly. Chop-chop.

JEMIMA: Nonsense. Give her a glass of champagne.

LESLIE: There isn't any.

JEMIMA: Of course there is—for Lena. It's just those *other* monsters. Don't just stand there, Leslie, open the bottle! *I* feel like it now. (*She adjusts herself comfortably on her chair, prepared to play hostess at last.*) And stop calling the author 'Miss'.

LESLIE: What should I call her—ms?

JEMIMA: Lena, of course. 'Miss' sounds unfriendly.

LESLIE: Really? Sorry, madam, I'm sure. (*Opens champagne.*) There you are, Lena.

(*Pours glass.* LENA *takes it, again as if he were not there.* LESLIE *hooks a glance across at* JEMIMA.)

Shall I fill you up again, madam, as the bishop said?

JEMIMA: Might as well get a bit sloshed before the real bores arrive.

LENA: You mean *I'm* not a real one?

JEMIMA: Not you, darling. But Leslie, if they're not all out by a quarter past eleven, interrupt and remind me out loud that I've—oh, I've got to have supper with the management or, oh, a film producer, *some*thing—

LESLIE: I'll think of something. Don't *I* get offered any champagne?

JEMIMA: Help yourself, stupid. See how I treat him? No one else would give him a job.

LESLIE: (*To* LENA) Well, it's just that I have this fetish thing going about ladies' brassieres. Can't help myself. And

24

madam here's got a lovely collection, haven't you madam? Can't hear, poor soul, it's the years of applause, affected the eardrums. Still, she never listens to anyone so no matter then. But she's a real lady, you know, she may not always behave like it but underneath there's real stock. Always tell real stock whatever position you find them in, legs in the air, on their back, any old where. No pride in real gentry, that's what my dear mother always used to say. Did your mother ever say anything like that?

(LENA *looks impatient and is about to speak to* JEMIMA.)

I'll bet she did. You *know* about these things. I can tell. I know your sort. *Deep.* That's what you are. Deep.

(JEMIMA *senses that this sending up of* LENA *won't do.*)

JEMIMA: Shut up, Leslie.

LESLIE: Very. Deep.

JEMIMA: And hang up my third act dress properly.

LENA: I popped in tonight.

LESLIE: Yes. We heard you.

LENA: What?

LESLIE: Laughing.

LENA: Oh? Was I?

LESLIE: You was.

LENA: Oh, I expect it was that new bit of business of Jemima's. You do it *so* marvellously. It was *such* a good idea.

JEMIMA: It seems to work.

LESLIE: Anything for a laugh. 'Takes off from the Theatre of the Absurd and drags it screaming back into the bourgeois bedroom. Brilliant and Original.'—*Sunday Times.*

LENA: Actually, it was the *Observer.*

LESLIE: Sorry, miss. More champagne?

(LENA *takes it.*)

LENA: Are you going to New York with the play?

JEMIMA: I'm not sure yet.

LENA: Oh, *do* go. You'll be a triumph. Even if the play's a flop.

LESLIE: In New York you can't be a triumph in a flop. Only in London. Americans think failure is contagious and if you've been anywhere near it, they might catch it. Poor souls.

Madam?

JEMIMA: Yes?

LESLIE: Can I go home please, milady? I've got a hot guardsman waiting for me in the oven.

JEMIMA: Of course you can't.

LENA: Oh, let him go. I think I've written another part for you in my new play.

LESLIE: Another!

LENA: I brought it with me for you to read.

LESLIE: The Edgar Wallace of the Theatre Upstairs aren't we? (*A knock at the door.*)

JEMIMA: There you are! They're coming after all. Damn!

LENA: I thought we could have half an hour together alone. Or you might let me take you out to supper.

LESLIE: Matinée tomorrow.

JEMIMA: See who it is and see if you can't get rid of them.

LESLIE: I'll try.

JEMIMA: Well, try harder!

(LESLIE *opens the door and they listen as he talks to someone in the corridor outside.*)

LESLIE: Just a minute . . . It's a Dr Grove.

JEMIMA: Ronald! Come *in*! Darling. Have you been outside long?

(*Ronald enters.*)

RONALD: The stage doorman's a bit fierce.

JEMIMA: Sit down. Have a drink. Leslie! What will you have? Champagne! Leslie! Open another bottle!

LESLIE: But—

JEMIMA: We're going to need it.

LESLIE: All right then.

JEMIMA: Darling Ronnie! How are you? Have you been in that place of yours, where is it, Portugal?

RONALD: Yes.

JEMIMA: You look terrific, Ronnie, I'm sorry, this is Lena Rogers, the author, of the play.

RONALD: How do you do. I thought it was very interesting.

LESLIE: Cautious!

26

RONALD: Congratulations. (*To* JEMIMA.) I thought you were marvellous. Razor's edge all the way.

JEMIMA: That's the author.

LESLIE: It's madam's sublime artistry. That's what the Princess Royal whispered to me, anyway.

RONALD: I've been away on a lecture tour in South America and the States so I didn't see it when you opened. What is it now? Ten months you've been running?

LENA: Eleven.

LESLIE: And she's got the royalties to prove it.

RONALD: You are going to New York I suppose?

JEMIMA: I don't know yet. The play is. Fill up Lena's glass, Leslie, and stop being so bloody flirtatious.

LESLIE: Sorry, madam.

JEMIMA: Do I need to see *you*! I need some pills so badly!

RONALD: As usual.

(*A figure appears in the doorway. A young man about thirty.*)

JEMIMA: Leslie!

(LESLIE *goes to the door and bars the visitor's path.*)

LESLIE: Yes?

JEMIMA: My dear, the sleep thing is worse than ever and I've got a matinée again tomorrow. Got anything for my back? Even Leslie can't do much with it. What do you suppose it is? I play tennis at least three times a week. Who is it, Leslie?

LESLIE: Mr Stanley Klob.

(LESLIE *grins at* JEMIMA'S *look of irritation.*)

JEMIMA: Klob?

LESLIE: Klob. With a K. Of Seattle.

JEMIMA: I don't know anyone in Seattle.

LESLIE: No Klob?

JEMIMA: Get rid of him.

LESLIE: Right you are.

(*The young man anticipates* LESLIE *and is in the room before he can get to the door.*)

KLOB: Forgive me for intruding. I didn't know you were having a party.

JEMIMA: I'm not having a party.

KLOB: My name is Klob. Stanley Klob.

JEMIMA: I remember now. You left your card at the stage door last week.

KLOB: And the week before that.

JEMIMA: You did?

KLOB: Yes. You see, as you weren't able to see me, I delayed my return to the States. And then again this week.

JEMIMA: Good Heavens. (*Pause*) Did you see the play tonight?

KLOB: Oh, yes. I've seen it eight times now.

LESLIE: Eight!

KLOB: Six evening performances and two matinées. I'm coming tomorrow.

(*Pause*)

JEMIMA: It wasn't very good tonight. The audience was as thick as thickness.

KLOB: I didn't notice. Oh yes, there was one irritating woman who kept laughing in a very loud, sort of false way.

LESLIE: Champagne, Mr Klob?

KLOB: Oh, thank you, no. Do you have a Coke?

LESLIE: With *this* play, naturally.

JEMIMA: I'm sorry, Mr Klob, this is Miss Rogers.

KLOB: How do you do, Miss Rogers.

LESLIE: The author of the play, Mr Klob. One Coke.

KLOB: Oh no, really. I *am* honoured. You have written a very fine play, Miss Rogers. Let me congratulate you on having written a very fine play.

LENA: Thank you.

KLOB: Yes, indeed. A very thought-provoking piece of work if I may say so.

LESLIE: You'd better.

JEMIMA: Fill up Lena's glass.

KLOB: Each time I've seen it, I've detected different insights.

LESLIE: Well, you do. *I* do.

JEMIMA: And fill mine too. Oh and this is Dr Grove.

(KLOB *and* RONALD *shake hands.*)

KLOB: I must apologise for intruding on you and your friends.

LESLIE: Oh, it's Liberty Hall.

KLOB: Pardon? I just have a small request to make. I am doing a postgraduate course and I have undertaken—

LESLIE: A thesis?

KLOB: Why yes. On the resurgence of the English drama during the period nineteen-fifty to nineteen-seventy. And I wondered if I could prevail a little on your time, seeing that you played some part in that movement.

JEMIMA: Only a very small part.

LENA: Nonsense.

LESLIE: Hear, hear.

KLOB: I wondered if you might—

JEMIMA: Well, I'm filming all day at present and—

KLOB: Oh, I could always visit you at the studios. I could come every day and wait for you when you weren't actually on the set.

JEMIMA: Well, they're rather strict.

KLOB: I'm sure I could arrange something with the producer.

LESLIE: You bet.

JEMIMA: Leslie!

(*Another visitor has arrived. A teenage girl.* LESLIE *intercepts.*)

KLOB: What is the name of the film?

JEMIMA: It's untitled as yet.

KLOB: And the director?

JEMIMA: It keeps changing. I'm sure Miss Rogers would be more articulate than me. After all, she is really one of the very newest ones.

KLOB: Of course. I had her way up on my itinerary. May I ask you a question, Miss Rogers?

LENA: Please.

KLOB: Would it be safe to describe you as a socialist?

LENA: Yes.

KLOB: Marxist?

LENA: Yes.

KLOB: I see. And would you also say that you were militant Women's Lib?

LENA: Like most intelligent people, yes.

KLOB: And would you say that both themes form a running

counterpoint in your play?

LENA: Well . . .

KLOB: Do forgive me. But it is so exciting for me to meet and talk with you and in these special surroundings. Tell me, have you ever considered writing a play for the Gay Sweatshop?

LENA: Well . . .

LESLIE: Miss Shirley Rose.

JEMIMA: Who?

LESLIE: She'd like you to sign her copy of Mr Lamont's biography of you.

JEMIMA: Oh, all right.

(LESLIE *lets the girl into the room.*)

GIRL: Sorry to trouble you. If you'd just—

JEMIMA: Certainly.

LESLIE: She wants to be an actress.

JEMIMA: (*Taking the book from her*) Yes?

GIRL: Did you go to the RADA?

LESLIE: Madam started at the top. It's the only way if you're a genius.

KLOB: I think Mr Lamont is a very fine critic, don't you?

LENA: No.

KLOB: You don't?

LENA: I think he's a petty bourgeois, rigid, running-scared cripple. Like they all are.

KLOB: Really? Well, in the States, he's very highly regarded.

LENA: He would be.

KLOB: But then we only have Clive Barnes.

LESLIE: That shouldn't happen even to Gay Sweatshop.

(*Two more visitors have appeared. A middle-aged, very respectable couple.*)

Yes?

RONALD: It's obviously going to be a bit crowded. I'll give you a ring at the weekend.

JEMIMA: No—don't go, please. It won't be for long.

Anyway, I have to be in bed very early tonight. Yes?

LESLIE: Mr and Mrs Colbourne.

JEMIMA: Don't know them. Tell them, oh—yes?

MRS COLBOURNE: Jemima!

JEMIMA: I'm sorry?

MRS COLBOURNE: You don't recognise me!

JEMIMA: I'm afraid I don't.

MRS COLBOURNE: There!—I tried. Roger, my husband.

ROGER: How do you do. *Did* enjoy it.

MRS COLBOURNE: I suppose I've changed a lot since you last saw me? Well, we *were* both in gymslips and boaters.

JEMIMA: Gymslips?

LESLIE: Kinky!

MRS COLBOURNE: You haven't changed. It's incredible. But then you've lived a very different life. Both our eldest children are at boarding-school. You still don't know who I am, do you?

JEMIMA: No. I don't.

LESLIE: (*Softly*) It's her illegitimate daughter.

MRS COLBOURNE: Maresfield!

JEMIMA: Maresfield?

MRS COLBOURNE: Maresfield. The school. *Your* school. We were there at the same time. *Now* do you remember? We were in the Sixth together. Ethelburga! Ethelburga House. You were awfully good at lacrosse and rotten at hockey because you were afraid of hurting your legs.

LESLIE: Ethelburga. Madam—you should have *said*.

(JEMIMA *tries to hide her embarrassment at the spectacle of this squat, middle-aged woman in her suburban tweeds, hat and gloves, prattling on like an aged schoolgirl. She recovers.*)

JEMIMA: Of course! I remember now. You haven't really changed all that much. It's just that I haven't got my glasses on and I'm quite blind.

MRS COLBOURNE: Oh come, of course I have! But then when you get to *our* age, you can't expect things to be the same. Time makes its mark on all of us, even you—

(LESLIE *snorts an irredeemable snigger.*)

—though, as I say, you look quite remarkable. I said to Roger when the curtain went up, that's *her* all right! It's hard to think we were in the same form together.

JEMIMA: Will you both have a drink?

MRS COLBOURNE: Well, why not? I suppose it's something of a reunion after all these years.

JEMIMA: Well, it was very nice of you to come round.

MRS COLBOURNE: I just couldn't not. Roger didn't want to come. But I said I knew you'd be sure to be glad to see an old school chum. One just loses touch with people one was so close to even if it is when one was young. We all go our own ways and never hear again. It's very sad. But then one has a career, gets married, has children, or in your case—Do you have any children?

JEMIMA: No.

LESLIE: She's barren.

(MRS COLBOURNE *looks about to be shocked but seems to put it down to theatrical eccentricity.*)

MRS COLBOURNE: Do you remember Cynthia Riply?

JEMIMA: Yes. She had breath like a fetid flame-thrower and hair on her nipples like paint brushes.

MRS COLBOURNE: Such a nice girl. Super tennis player, wasn't she? Married into the Diplomatic almost immediately. Somewhere in the Indian Ocean. I see her about once a year when he's on leave. We have a girls' lunch together and talk about old times. It was she who told me about your being in the play. We only read the *Daily Telegraph* and I seem to miss that page about plays and things.

LESLIE: What will you have to drink, Mrs Colbourne?

MRS COLBOURNE: Oh, how nice! I'll have a dry sherry if I may.

LESLIE: Sir?

ROGER: Oh, whisky for me, old chap.

JEMIMA: May I introduce—

KLOB: Klob. Stanley Klob.

MRS COLBOURNE: How do you do.

JEMIMA: This young lady—

GIRL: Shirley Rose.

JEMIMA: Dr Grove . . . And this is Lena Rogers who wrote the play.

MRS COLBOURNE: Oh, how very nice! Fancy meeting the author! My husband and I *did* enjoy the play. Though I must say— you don't mind my saying it, do you—I was a wee bit dubious about some of the four-letter words and, well, some of the, well, *other* things? Still, *we* live such an ordinary sort of life and so I suppose we're a bit out of touch with these things, not like *you* people. We live a pretty quiet sort of life. Although we keep pretty busy. I dare say we seem a bit complacent, but there doesn't seem much to complain about.

LENA: I'll bet there isn't.

MRS COLBOURNE: No. You're right. We're very lucky. But you see today is our wedding anniversary. Nineteen years of Bash and Bliss. Isn't it, eh Boot?

ROGER: That's right, Petal.

MRS COLBOURNE: Roger usually likes to arrange everything, whatever it is. He says I've got no sense of organisation and I dare say he's right though I'd like to see him manage three strapping boys *and* look after him and entertain his friends. Then there's his mother. She's an absolute dear but crippled with arthritis and old people *can* be pretty demanding, however nice they are, can't they? Anyway. I said if we're going up to town why don't we have a quiet dinner, a bottle of champagne to ourselves and go to a show, and why not go and see Jemima?

JEMIMA: I see.

MRS COLBOURNE: He wanted to see the new James Bond as we don't often bother to go to the cinema. But I said come on, we haven't been for years and we'll still get the last train so that the baby sitter doesn't start kicking the television set. Oh, we *did* enjoy it. Did you?

RONALD: Yes. Very much.

MRS COLBOURNE: (*To* LENA) Didn't you think we were a frightfully good audience?

LENA: No.

MRS COLBOURNE: Oh? We thought we'd been rather special. I didn't even dare open the box of chocolates Roger gave me. Still, I suppose in *your* profession you can never be really

B

satisfied. You *know* about these things, things we ordinary public simply don't notice. Still, we just go to have a good time.

15. INTERIOR. NIGHT. DRESSING-ROOM

Pause.

LESLIE: Quite. Have a good time—even if it does make your eyes water. (*He turns to see a man in his thirties, dressed rather as if he were a flamboyant teenager.*) Oh, not you! Haven't you got a home, dear, or have they pulled down all the Gloucester Road cottages?

JEMIMA: (*Thrilled to stop* MRS COLBOURNE *for the moment*) Anthony!

ANTHONY: Darling!

(JEMIMA *and* ANTHONY *embrace—over-effusively perhaps.*)

LESLIE: Oh, Gawd! (*To* ROGER.) Pass me the sick bag.

JEMIMA: How *are* you?

ANTHONY: Well, that's what I came about. My dear, I've had the most ghastly week. I can't tell you.

JEMIMA: My darling, you must talk about it.

LESLIE: Don't worry—he will.

JEMIMA: Give him a drink.

ANTHONY: A large whisky and no ice, Leslie please.

LESLIE: We're not giving her drinks, are we? Some day I'm going to show you madam's drinks bill for this dressing-room.

ANTHONY: Ta. Oh, I've got to tell you—I've got the most divine little dog.

JEMIMA: No? Will you bring him in?

ANTHONY: Of course, I would have brought him in but he's only been away from his mummy for a week so he's still a bit miz. He just sits with me in the shop all day. You'll love him!

JEMIMA: What is he?

ANTHONY: A sealyham. White all over.

LESLIE: More than his new daddy.

ANTHONY: Oh, I needed that drink! I can't *tell* you!

JEMIMA: Sorry, Anthony, this is Mr and Mrs Colbourne, Ronald

34

you've met, Miss Rose and Lena, you know . . .

ANTHONY: Hi! (*Without much interest he nods quickly and turns back to* JEMIMA.) Apart from him—Rudi—after Rudolf you know—

LESLIE: Original!

ANTHONY: It's been a real bitch of a week. I longed to ring you up but you never seem to be in when I call. I've not slept for five nights.

JEMIMA: But why?

ANTHONY: Ernest!

LESLIE: Not shopped *again*!

ANTHONY: Well, not exactly, but I do think he's looking for big trouble. He met this feller at that place I took you to—

JEMIMA: Super.

ANTHONY: You wouldn't like it now, dear. Anyway, he comes home last weekend. I thought he'd been a bit moody, and suddenly, we were having a drink and watching Bette in *Jezebel*—isn't she fan*tastic* when she comes in in the Red Dress! Henry Fonda wasn't half fanciable then, I'd forgotten—so, there we are, all relaxed *I* thought and he bursts into tears. And it started to come *out* . . . Grisly! So, I turned off the film—I had to, he was in such a state, and we never got to bed all night.

JEMIMA: Poor Ernest!

LESLIE: (*To* MRS COLBOURNE *softly*) Poor *tart*! Where is he? Should I ring him up?

ANTHONY: I haven't seen him for two days. I've been *everywhere*.

LESLIE: Except the police.

ANTHONY: What are you doing next? Why don't we have a steak sandwich somewhere and a bit of a jig? It would cheer us both up.

JEMIMA: I really can't, darling—

ANTHONY: Come on, she's nearly dressed, isn't she, Leslie?

JEMIMA: I've got a matinée, Anthony. How many times do I have to tell you? (*Pointedly at them all.*) I've got two shows tomorrow and after that shower we had in tonight, I just want a cup of Ovaltine and go to bed.

ANTHONY: Oh, come on. You'll be all right. You're a night person, like me.

JEMIMA: No, really! (*Getting a bit irritable.*) People seem to think one's got endless energy. Well, I've got so much but sometimes I need it for myself! (*Slight pause. She sees a woman, about her own age, at the door.*) Susan!

SUSAN: Hello, Jemima.

(JEMIMA *and* SUSAN *embrace rather perfunctorily.*)

JEMIMA: Susan! What are you doing here? Don't tell me you were out front?

SUSAN: Yes, I was actually.

JEMIMA: But how awful. We were just saying what a rotten house they were.

SUSAN: Usual West End audience I thought.

JEMIMA: You didn't come on your own!

SUSAN: No. (*Beside her is a dark, tanned young man with very carefully styled hair and wearing a long, expensive fur coat.*) This is René.

JEMIMA: Hallo. You should have told me.

SUSAN: I only came at the last minute. I wanted to get out of the house so we thought we'd come and see you in your play.

JEMIMA: Did you like it?

SUSAN: No.

JEMIMA: Oh! Well, I could see why you wouldn't . . . What about you, René?

SUSAN: He slept.

JEMIMA: Doesn't he talk?

SUSAN: Yes. But only French.

JEMIMA: Well, of course, that's very French isn't it? I saw about the divorce today. Has it been horrid?

SUSAN: Usual. Gossip columnists ringing up in the middle of the night and going through my dustbins in the daytime.

JEMIMA: Charming, aren't they?

SUSAN: If you're a public figure like Ted, you're public property, isn't that what they say? He'd very stupidly gone to some trendy restaurant with his new girl, showing her off, I

36

suppose, and then he's surprised when some charmer tips off the Press.

JEMIMA: What's she like? Dim little scrubber I suppose.

SUSAN: No, I've met her. She's very nice and intelligent actually. She adores him quite genuinely I think. She's not overawed by him but she's kindly, which is more than most of them are.

JEMIMA: Really? You do surprise me. Still, Ted always wanted a farmer's-wife-mother-type really. That's why you and I were no good to him.

SUSAN: We were certainly inadequate. I've come to see that about both of us.

JEMIMA: *Have* you? (*She is finding it hard to conceal her dislike from the others. She turns to them.*) I'm so sorry. This is all a bit complicated, I'm afraid. Give Susan and her friend a drink, will you, Leslie? This is Mrs Lang. And she was married to *my* ex-husband, Edward Lang. That is to say, she *was*, until today. She's come to celebrate—like you (*To* MRS COLBOURNE:)—to celebrate. Only it's her second divorce instead of her nineteenth wedding anniversary.

MRS COLBOURNE: I think I read about it.

LESLIE: There were photographs all over the papers. 'Edward Lang just divorced dines out with his new-found companion, Miss Tooting Bec.'

MRS COLBOURNE: We only get the *Telegraph* I'm afraid. Is your husband famous, Mrs Lang?

SUSAN: He's famous for being famous.

JEMIMA: I'm sorry you didn't like the play. You must meet the author. She likes a bit of hard-hitting discussion about her work. That's her over there. Oh, I'm so sorry. This is Mr and Mrs Colbourne, Mr Klob, Miss er—

GIRL: Rose.

JEMIMA: Rose. Dr Grove, Leslie, you know of course.

SUSAN: Hallo, Leslie. How's tricks?

LESLIE: Disaster time, dear. Evening, Freddie. (*A short, middle-aged man in owlish spectacles has entered. He has a withered arm.*) Filed your notice or whatever it is you do with that

37

vicious stuff you write about us poor little artistes?

FREDDIE: Evening, Leslie. Jemima, my dear.

JEMIMA: Freddie, darling! What a nice surprise! Have you just been to the first night?

FREDDIE: Looking lovely. Yes, just turned in my vicious piece, as Leslie says.

JEMIMA: Was it awful?

FREDDIE: Dreadful.

JEMIMA: I knew it must be. With that cast and *her*! Did she still do that funny walk as if she's got her loving fingers up her own arse?

FREDDIE: Something like that.

JEMIMA: Tell me more. What about the play? *I* turned it down, I told you.

FREDDIE: You can read it tomorrow.

LESLIE: There goes a dozen poor little devils' jobs. Usual?

FREDDIE: Please, Leslie. I wanted to have a word with you about the old biography. It's done incredibly well.

JEMIMA: Goody!

FREDDIE: So much so that they want to bring it out in paperback and they've asked me to bring a few things up to date and add an extensive appendix.

JEMIMA: How marvellous! Me—in paperback! You should have waited, Miss Rose. You could have got it for half the price. I'm so sorry, this is Frederic Lamont, the critic.

FREDDIE: How do you do?

JEMIMA: Miss Rose. I've just signed a copy of her book.

FREDDIE: Hang on to it then. You'll be able to put it up at Christie's one day.

(*He waves his stumpy arm and kisses* JEMIMA.)

JEMIMA: Mr and Mrs Colbourne. Mr Klob from Seattle. Dr Grove. And, well, you know one another . . .

FREDDIE: Anything new for us?

JEMIMA: Yes, but I doubt *you're* ready for it.

FREDDIE: Don't be so sure. It was *my* extra vote got you the *Evening Standard* Best Play Award. And quite right too.

SUSAN: Pretty bourgeois bauble to give a left-winger ladies' lady author I'd have thought.

FREDDIE: Not at all. We're going to see greater things than ever from this young lady. Take my word.

LESLIE: Don't. He's the highest paid critic in Fleet Street. Arnold Bennett's not in it! Here, Freddie. Oh, my Gawd, what have we got here?

(*During all this a group of yet more visitors has appeared, and from now on it is a non-stop influx. The room gets noisier and noisier until, eventually, people are having to shout and* JEMIMA *is left at her dressing-table, fully dressed and no one taking any notice of her.* LESLIE *is pouring drinks and refilling them endlessly.*)

16. INTERIOR. NIGHT. DRESSING-ROOM

The room is really packed now and LESLIE *is sweating at the drinks table, the air is thick with smoke and yet more people try to get in the door.* JEMIMA *is pinned against her dressing-table in the press. Some people look at her and others bend down and greet her briefly. She can hardly hear.*

JEMIMA: Leslie. Get me a drink! After all, I *did* pay for it. Oh—bed!

17. INTERIOR. NIGHT. DRESSING-ROOM

LESLIE *refilling drinks.*

LESLIE: Talk about Royal Garden Party! (*To* ANTHONY.) *You* could give me a hand instead of rabbiting on about Ernest!

18. INTERIOR. NIGHT. DRESSING-ROOM

KLOB: I've read your biography several times and there are one or two points I would like to take up with you.

FREDDIE: Of course.

KLOB: I expect you know that you are very much admired in the States. Of course, we do have Clive Barnes.

FREDDIE: Sound chap.

SUSAN: On the contrary, he's a fat, deviating slob, a third-rate ballet reviewer masquerading as a tenth-rate Broadway Butcher.

39

LENA: (*To* SUSAN) I'm sorry you didn't like my play.

FREDDIE: That's a bit harsh and overstated, Mrs Lang.

SUSAN: So is all this.

FREDDIE: What?

SUSAN: (*Shouting above din*) I say so is all this. (*To* LENA.) Why should you care what *I* think? These people all think you're great. Maybe you are.

19. INTERIOR. NIGHT. DRESSING-ROOM

MRS COLBOURNE: She must get so tired, night after night saying the same old thing for months on end! She's looking a bit frail, don't you think?

RONALD: She's as strong as a tank.

MRS COLBOURNE: Really? She was never very good at games. But very brainy. We all thought she was going to be a vet or something like that. We never would have thought we'd see her name up in lights when she was in Ethelburga's. Of course, you're a doctor, aren't you? We have an awfully good doctor for Roger's mother, you know. Oh, yes, we did quite enjoy it. It seems you can say anything on the stage these days, or anywhere for that matter. Still, as I say, we like to lead a quiet life don't we, Boot? Still, you did enjoy it, didn't you?

ROGER: Not my sort of thing really. Bit unnecessary some of it, I thought. Still, the last good show I saw was *South Pacific*.

MRS COLBOURNE: Oh, that was divine! Can't remember who we saw in it.

20. INTERIOR. NIGHT. DRESSING-ROOM

ANTHONY: I had to take him in a taxi round to the casualty department and we waited for hours. And Ernest was still in agony. I said to the nurse 'can't you see this man is in agony!' 'Aren't we all?' she said.

GIRL: Are these all her friends?

ANTHONY: What? Of course, dear. Jemima's got more friends than you've had hot dinners.

21. INTERIOR. NIGHT. DRESSING-ROOM

LENA: Well, tell me then.

SUSAN: Well, for a start, it's glib, it's like most women's writing, begging your libbing pardon, it's pre-packed, lifeless-instant-life, fashionable left-wing-fascist, with one eye on the heavy press who are terrified they might miss out on a genuine talent but don't know the difference between boulevard dross like yours and the real painful thing and the other eye on that herd out there in the stalls. I—

LENA: Go on.

SUSAN: Right. All those tiresome assumptions about the selfless probity of the working-classes, it's sentimental, slack and undramatic warmed-over Lenin. You affect to despise the bourgeoisie who are mostly more interesting than your lot, forgetting that Chekhov wrote about nothing else and that Marx was a petit bourgeois intellectual soak who never saw a revolutionary shot fired in anger in his life. . . .

22. INTERIOR. NIGHT. DRESSING-ROOM

MRS COLBOURNE: Is this play Jemima's doing, you say, for BBC or ITV?

GIRL: ITV.

MRS COLBOURNE: Ah, we never watch ITV, or hardly ever, do we, Boot? We watch BBC sometimes and Nanny used to be glued to it, of course, but it's mostly for sport because Roger's very keen on that.

GIRL: Don't you ever watch plays?

MRS COLBOURNE: I don't think we do really, do we, Boot? Somehow we just don't seem to get the time, it's amazing. We've got three boys, you see. Of course, two of them are at Bryanston, the eldest is going up to Cambridge next year, he's reading Law and Jeremy, he's our baby, got a scholarship to Winchester.

GIRL: I tried to get a grant to the RADA.

MRS COLBOURNE: (*Uninterested*) Did you? It must be *so* boring for them, saying the same thing night after night, over and over again. I'd go quite mad. I don't know what makes them do

41

it! It does seem an odd life to *choose* when you don't have
to. Doesn't it? I mean, well, over and over . . .

23. INTERIOR. NIGHT. DRESSING-ROOM
JEMIMA *hemmed in by crowd. A man treads on her foot.*
MAN: Oh—sorry. Didn't see you.
   (JEMIMA *pushes him in the back but he doesn't notice.*)
GIRL: I say, where's the loo?
JEMIMA: Down the corridor.
GIRL: Thanks.
JEMIMA: Don't mention it. I only live here.

24. INTERIOR. NIGHT. DRESSING-ROOM
ROGER: Er. Pourquoi—er pourquoi vous n'aimez pas parler
   Anglais. Est-ce que c'est trop difficile ou—
RENÉ: She just says it to make people laugh and stop me saying
   something embarrassing.
ROGER: Oh. What's your line of business then? You're not in this
   game too, are you?
RENÉ: Game?

25. INTERIOR. NIGHT. DRESSING-ROOM
SUSAN: She nearly killed him with all this crapola. Ted.
RONALD: Crapola?
SUSAN: Sure. And I wasn't much better. Good luck to him with
   Miss Tooting Bec, I say.
RONALD: Why do you dislike her so much?
   (FREDDIE'*s stumpy arm waving.*)
SUSAN: (*At* FREDDIE) I wish he wouldn't wave that thing in the
   air.

26. INTERIOR. NIGHT. DRESSING-ROOM
JEMIMA, *fully dressed, is edging her way out of the room. She forces
her way out, waving at* LESLIE, *who winks at her over the glasses.*
JEMIMA: (*To sprawling young man*) Excuse me.
YOUNG MAN: Help yourself.

27. INTERIOR. NIGHT. DRESSING-ROOM
Clamour louder than ever.

SUSAN: Because she's cold-hearted, mean-spirited, not very bright, witty about the discomfort of others but humourless, ruthless, ambitious about her talent, which is not all she and others crack it up to be, spoilt, man-hating, *un*generous to a fault, reads nothing but gush about diets, vitamin E, skin care, other actors' bad notices, clothes, crimpers, her queer minions and various eunuchs because she's incapable of anything real or difficult or not self-promoting . . .

RONALD: Where is she, by the way?

SUSAN: Who cares? . . .

FREDDIE: You see it was never explained. We are never quite sure, we are never *told* why he behaves like this . . .

LENA: That doesn't stop you being a socialist. Use any means to get what you want. The rest is liberal crap . . .

MRS COLBOURNE: Well, we've only got an acre and a half. But that's more than enough for Roger to manage and I do what I can, don't I, Boot? . . .

GIRL: I'd do anything, absolutely anything just to get a start. I only want a *start*.

(The voices become indistinguishable. A blur altogether.)

28. EXTERIOR. NIGHT. SHAFTESBURY AVENUE
JEMIMA *gets into her car and it drives off.*

29. EXTERIOR. NIGHT. SHAFTESBURY AVENUE
A man tries to hail a taxi. It is quiet now, shabby. A water-cart passes. The lights of the theatres flicker.

Try a Little Tenderness

CAST

TED

KIM

DEBBIE

WINIFRED

ROBERT

SLIM

DE WITT

REV. DUCKWORTH

MISS BASTAPLE

LADY ARKLEY

GROUP-CAPTAIN HEFFER

BOLAS

MRS STRINGER

MR BALDOCK

MRS YEO

MRS GLOVER

SGT BROUGH

SAM (LANDLORD)

MR BENSON

MR DUFFARD

LARRY BEST

1. EXTERIOR. DAY
Aerial shot of English countryside looking very serene in autumn sunshine. Below can be made out the clear pattern of a traditional English village.

The downland is dotted with hill sheep, the lanes are in golden leaf and only a few cars can be seen on the larger roads. In the valley cows are grazing and tractors can be seen making their lines on the earth.

2. EXTERIOR. DAY
The same view from the ground. For miles around the scene is the same, frozen in misty tranquillity. Birds sing and from the cliff tops a few miles away gulls come and hover over the lakes and ponds.

3. EXTERIOR. DAY. FIELD
Some farmworkers are working.

4. EXTERIOR. DAY
TED, *a large man, about fifty, is leaning over a gate watching them. He is dressed in a slightly eccentric, old-fashioned, bohemian manner. Careless but somewhat calculated too. He waves his pipe at the men and moves off down the deserted lane towards the nearby village. His dog, Colditz, follows him happily.*

5. EXTERIOR. DAY. ST MICHAEL AND ST GEORGES CHURCH, ARKLEY. LYCH GATE
The vicar, the REV. STANLEY DUCKWORTH, *gets on to his bicycle and spins down the road into Arkley.*

49

6. EXTERIOR. DAY. DOG AND RABBIT FORECOURT

The local cub meet is assembling. Lots of shouts, calling out of names, 'Roger, Sarah', etc. Usual things. DUCKWORTH *waves at them, then at* TED, *who has stopped to watch.*

7. EXTERIOR. DAY. DOG AND RABBIT

The meet is almost prepared for the off. TED *turns to* DE WITT, *a sombre-looking gentleman, who has been talking eagerly to the Joint Master.*

TED: Not going out today, Master?

DE WITT: Can't. Drummond's sprained his hip, and, anyway, I've got to chair the meeting again. Damned little good it'll do at this last minute. They'll be *here* any minute! Ridiculous idea of yours if I may say so. Surprised the committee voted for it.

TED: So am I when I think of what most of them think of me.

DE WITT: What's that?

TED: Remember what Hugh Gaitskell said.

DE WITT: Who?

TED: Fight, fight, fight and fight again!

DE WITT: Said that did he? Well, must go and prepare the minutes. Can't trust that woman Bastaple. See you then. At the meeting.

TED: At the meeting.

(DE WITT *strides off. An aged man, clearly a farm labourer, approaches* TED. MR BALDOCK.)

MR BALDOCK: Expecting trouble?

TED: Don't know. We'll see when they get here. *They're* looking a bit more bloodthirsty than usual. Only going out for a short while, I hear.

MR BALDOCK: All piss and fart most of 'em. They pretend they can have all their own way, and we let 'em get away with it. But they know really, they can't stop things changing all the time. And they'll just have to get used to it.

TED: Yes. Depends on what the changes are, Mr Baldock. You and I think one way about most things and they think another. But there are some occasions when you have to join hands with your natural enemies.

MR BALDOCK: Well, I'm *for* anything they're agin!

TED: So am I, usually. At least, I think I so.

(*The Hunt moves off and* MR BALDOCK *and* TED *move smartly out of its way. One or two of the members acknowledge* TED *but most look rather chilly.*)

See you at the Crown.

MR BALDOCK: Right.

TED: You haven't forgotten what I asked you?

MR BALDOCK: No.

TED: Will you still do it?

MR BALDOCK: I reckon so. If you get that lot to agree. And that'll take a bit of doin' with *them*!

8. EXTERIOR. DAY. GENERAL STORES

'*Yeo* GENERAL STORES' *above the shop front. The doorbell rings and* TED *enters.* MRS YEO *is serving a customer.*

MRS YEO: Morning, Mr Shilling.

TED: Morning, Mrs Yeo.

MRS YEO: Be right with you. Only we're closing at dinner time today in case there's any trouble.

CUSTOMER: I think everyone is, till they've gone. Mr Bedford. The Crown is definitely closing though they say the Dog may stay open for a bit unless something happens.

MRS YEO: Fred's putting some old shutters up. But I told him no shutters is going to keep out their sort.

CUSTOMER: That's why I thought I'd stock up for a few days.

TED: Expecting a siege, Mrs Glover?

MRS GLOVER: Well, no, but you never know these days. They don't care what they do. *You* should know, invading your home and nobody able to do anything about it, not even people like you!

(*Enter* SGT BROUGH *of the local constabulary.*)

No one can. Not even the police. Not these days. The law's helpless. There's nothing even *they* can do about it. Not any of us can. They can all just do as they like and we're just helpless, helpless!

SGT BROUGH: Morning, Mrs Yeo, Mrs Glover, Mr Shilling.

MRS YEO: Morning, Sergeant. Right with you.

SGT BROUGH: No hurry.

MRS GLOVER: All police leave cancelled, I hear.

SGT BROUGH: Well, that's only me, Mrs Glover.

MRS GLOVER: But they're bringing in reinforcements from the County Constabulary. And they say there's a whole lot down from London as well. There's dozens of vans in the pound at Cowbridge, in the sports ground, everywhere.

SGT BROUGH: Just precautions, Mrs Glover. Just routine precautions.

MRS GLOVER: Got dogs, tear gas, modern devices.

TED: Are you expecting any trouble, Sergeant?

SGT BROUGH: No, I don't think so. They're used to handling these situations by now. No reason why it shouldn't go off quite smoothly if people don't lose their heads and I don't see why they should.

MRS YEO: What about the tax-payers' money, that's what I say. They come here and make life hell for us for days and *we* pay for it. Police dogs and all.

SGT BROUGH: You've a point there, Mrs Yeo. But I don't think there's much point in stopping people enjoying themselves harmlessly.

MRS GLOVER: So long as it *is* harmless. Why don't the police go along to Mr Shilling's house here and get those dirty ruffians out of Mr Shilling's house? Eh? Tell me! Squatters!

MRS YEO: Think they're a lot of Robin Hoods.

MRS GLOVER: You ask Mr Shilling. Filthy lot, making a mess, ruining that house. And he made *so* many improvements to it!

MRS YEO: I don't know—people like Mr Shilling, distinguished man, decides to get away from London after working hard all his life and get away from all the noise and dirt and come to a place where it's quiet and peaceful and people are decent and just get on with their own business and what happens? It follows him all the way down to a lovely little place like this!

SGT BROUGH: Well, there's some things we can do and some, it seems, we can't. It's all being looked into, I dare say.

MRS GLOVER: Well, it needs looking into pretty fast then—before we all go out of our minds.

MRS YEO: I agree. It's got really out of hand these past ten years or so. First we had them Swinging Sixties—whatever they meant by *that*. Now, it's going to be the Squatting Seventies from the look of it.

MRS GLOVER: And it's only just *started*! That's how it started with Hitler.

MRS YEO: Mrs Shilling says they don't use the toilets properly half the time.

TED: Well, they do seem to have got that a bit more organised. They're just a bit more casual about these things than perhaps you and I are.

MRS GLOVER: Casual! Barbaric I call it. I daren't think of what your lovely curtains and carpets must be like by now!

MRS YEO: And I *daren't* think of what that lovely bathroom suite they had put in must be like by now, Mrs Glover. Not that *they'd* bother with a bath!

TED: I dare say they'll get out sometime fairly soon. They'll get bored with the scene, man, and fold up and go to the next place, like gypsies.

MRS GLOVER: I wish they were half as good as gypsies even.

MRS YEO: And you know what Hitler did with *them*.

TED: My son lives with them in their part of the house.

MRS GLOVER: *Their* part of the house!

TED: That's how they see it. And that's how my son, Robert, sees it.

MRS GLOVER: Your own son! You mean he agrees with letting his beautiful house be ruined by these people!

TED: We'll clean it up when they've gone. They won't stay. Even Robert is bored, even more bored than he ever is with his parents.

MRS GLOVER: His own father! I know what Mr Glover would do if our boy tried anything like that. All I can say is, you're a very patient man, Mr Shilling.

SGT BROUGH: It's been hard on Mr Shilling, I agree, and it's been worse for him than anyone and he's complained less.

TED: Married men have to be patient, Sergeant, as you know. Until a certain point.

SGT BROUGH: Indeed I do! Oh, it'll all blow over, you see. Things like Hitler don't happen in England.

TED: (*Softly*) There's Mr De Witt.

MRS YEO: (*Laughing*) Now, Mr Shilling, I heard that! You're being wicked again!

TED: And the Group Captain.

SGT BROUGH: Young people's young people any time.

MRS GLOVER: These aren't young people. I think we *have* reached a certain point, whatever Mr Shilling means by that.

TED: I'm not absolutely sure yet.

SGT BROUGH: I reckon they're not half as black as they're painted. I've not seen much down here, naturally, but from what I read and see on the television they're a pretty quiet, harmless lot. Mark you, if there's any trouble it will be from *our* people.

MRS YEO: Who?

SGT BROUGH: The locals.

MRS GLOVER: But who?

SGT BROUGH: Certain elements. I can't say who. But they're under surveillance.

MRS GLOVER: Oh! Really.

MRS YEO: Yes, now, Mr Shilling?

TED: I've got a big order, Mrs Yeo. It's one of my cooking days.

MRS GLOVER: Cooking days?

TED: Yes, I usually do some cooking when I think I may make some decisions. I find decisions almost impossible—and cooking soothes the brain, sends the blood rushing to the sinews gently and nice and pleasantly . . . I want a lot of leeks and onions and other things so you'd better serve the Sergeant first.

SGT BROUGH: Thank you. I just want some stamps and a registered envelope please.

MRS GLOVER: Well, I can only say: you're a very patient man, a very patient man, Mr Shilling.

TED: No, I'm not, Mrs Glover. I'm not patient at all, alas. I just know how to wait and when to strike. When to strike—it's the heart beat of all art. It's my mother-in-law's eighty-ninth birthday today.

MRS YEO: Oh, how nice.

TED: Yes. I think it might turn out quite well. I think certain special occasions are good for making fresh decisions.

MRS GLOVER: Yes. I suppose they might be.

TED: I've made her a special chocolate cake.

MRS YEO: Oh, that's nice.

TED: I hope so. She loves chocolate cake. So does my wife. They both have an appetite for the sweets of life.

MRS YEO: Oh yes?

TED: Provided they don't have to make or provide them.

MRS GLOVER: Like them squatters.

TED: Very like.

9. INTERIOR. DAY. THE CROWN

The LANDLORD *is behind the bar, talking to* TED *and* BALDOCK.

LANDLORD: Well, I'm not having any of 'em come in here.

BALDOCK: You'll lose a lot of trade, Sam.

LANDLORD: I don't care. All they drink is Coke and soft drinks. All they like is smoking that pot stuff—like that lot up at *your* place.

TED: Sergeant Brough's been up twice with the Cowbridge police dogs and all, and found nothing.

LANDLORD: I don't care. They'll be having some, you see! They can't get off it once they're hooked. And when they do, you'll be the first to smell it, being in the same house, and if you take my advice, you'll stop being soft-hearted and tell the police right away. They'll drop on 'em like a ton of bricks.

TED: They know that, they're not stupid.

LANDLORD: But their brains get addled, what with not working and listening to that tripe all day and night. Enough to make anyone take even more risks. And old Brough tells me soon as they do, they'll drop on 'em like a ton of bricks. Just drop on 'em. They're only waiting. You see. You've been too soft-hearted and meek all along with this business, Ted. You want to defend your rights and stand up and be counted.

TED: But who with? That's what makes it difficult.

LANDLORD: Who with?

TED: Well, I agree with a lot of people but I often don't agree with the *people* I agree with.

LANDLORD: Rubbish. Right's right, whoever agrees with it.

BALDOCK: That's like the end justifies the means.

LANDLORD: Well, they won't get inside *this* pub. This place is closed to everyone until that lot is back on the road to London—even to you and Ted.

BALDOCK: What about the Dog?

LANDLORD: Old Sid says he may open. He doesn't want to but old De Witt and his pals are trying to pressure him to open just for them. And you know what *they* are. Those sort of people always get their own way in the end. They always have done and they always will. But they can't bully me, not those old admirals and Lady this and that. Sid's a bit on the weak side with that sort. You've got to be strong or you'll get no respect from *that* kind.

TED: Well, I must go off and get the lunch.

LANDLORD: What, again? Doesn't your wife ever do no cooking for you, Ted?

TED: Sometimes. But I enjoy it and it doesn't interest her.

LANDLORD: And what does interest her then?

TED: I often ask that question myself. See you at the barricades then. 'Bye. Come on, Colditz. (*He goes out, followed by the dog.*)

LANDLORD: Too soft-hearted that's what he is. Let himself get trampled on, he will. Strange for someone so clever.

BALDOCK: He just bides his time.

LANDLORD: He'd better buck up then. What with that mother-in-law and that son of theirs. And his girl friend. And that couple who are her friends, the wife I mean, *they're* still

56

staying with them. The husband's not so bad. But she's a bossy little rat-bag. And now there's this ballet dancer friend of hers and his friend. I don't know. He seems to look after the lot, single-handed.

BALDOCK: My uncle said if you learn to serve you're half-way to being in command.

10. EXTERIOR. DAY. VILLAGE STREET

DE WITT *strides along. Several people say good morning to him. He just about acknowledges them. He approaches the Village Hall. Above the doorway is a sign 'Keep the Festival Out—Committee Rooms. Emergency Meeting. 4.15.' He stops as a chauffeur-driven Daimler of not too recent vintage comes to a leisurely halt. From it steps an old lady,* LADY ARKLEY, *holding a cane but not too creaky not to look quite fierce, which she does.* DE WITT *helps her down.*

LADY ARKLEY: I can manage. Don't fuss, George.

DE WITT: Good morning, Nora.

LADY ARKLEY: I can't see that it's going to be very *good*!

11. EXTERIOR. DAY. VILLAGE STREET

TED *and Colditz stop outside the Butcher's, 'Benson, Family Butchers. Home Killed'.*

TED: Morning, Mr Benson.

BENSON: Morning to you, sir. Nice day for a bit of music.

TED: Lovely. Mind if Colditz comes in?

BENSON: 'Course not. Come in for a bone have you, old boy? The wife says we'll be good and fed up by Monday. But I don't mind a bit of music. Even if it is a bit on the loud side, like they say. But life *is* loud these days, isn't it? Since them Beatles and all that. People don't *want* peace and quiet no more. That's all the modern trend, isn't it? They want something a bit lively, what with all these strikes, and violence and rape and all that.

TED: Still, I suppose strikes and rape can be pretty lively, too.

BENSON: Ah well, you got a point there, sir. Still I reckon some of these people are making a bit of a fuss about nothing very

57

much if you ask me. What is it—just a bit of noise and inconvenience that's all. People like Lady Arkley, they go on like it was the end of the world.

TED: Perhaps it *is* the end of theirs.

BENSON: Maybe, and not such a bad thing, I'd say. 'Ad it all their own way too long too some of 'em. Now they find they can't pop the ferret down the 'ole any longer. Not much longer they can't.

TED: They're trying.

BENSON: Oh, they'll try all right. They always do. But time and tide, time and tide. Though I never thought it would catch up to Arkley.

TED: Will you be opening or closing up like most of the shopkeepers?

BENSON: They're getting into such a panic some of 'em, you'd think they was like them whites in Rhodesia. Well, we don't open Monday anyway. Now, what can I do for you, sir?

TED: Did you get me that large bacon bone?

BENSON: I did, sir. Right here.

TED: And the garlic sausage?

BENSON: Had to send up for that. Came this morning. What you cooking up this time, then?

TED: Cassoulet.

BENSON: What's that then?

TED: A sort of French peasants' stew. It's my mother-in-law's birthday.

BENSON: Does she like that sort of thing then?

TED: I don't think so. But I do.

BENSON: She'd like something more of a curry wouldn't she, being out East all those years?

TED: You couldn't make that old Bridge-bag's eyes water with anything.

BENSON: (*Laughs*) That's right. You give 'em what *you* like! Here we are then. Can't say I'd like to eat it myself. Still, some people do say it's very nice once you get the taste for it.

TED: I'll bring you some.

BENSON: Well, thank you.

TED: They're sure to leave it.

(BENSON *laughs*.)

BENSON: You got quite a bit on your hands up there, I should think, what with your squatters or whatever it is they call 'em.

TED: Yes. But I'm coping.

BENSON: I'm sure, knowing you. I hear Mrs Shilling's got another couple of visitors. Some ballet dancer gentleman and his friend.

TED: That's right.

BENSON: That'll be nice for her.

TED: Seems so.

BENSON: Not much for a lady like your wife to do in a little place like this, really. She must miss giving up all that ballet dancing, I imagine.

TED: She does. Very much. But when people say they gave something up for something else, I always wonder what it was exactly they gave up. It's not always the jewel they give you to think.

BENSON: Yes. Well, it's all hard competition in that world, I believe. Non-stop.

TED: Endless . . . self-seeking ambition.

BENSON: Ambition, you're right, sir. Still, it's what some people wants. Can't say I can see it can always be worth all that trouble.

TED: It isn't.

BENSON: Still, it'll be nice for her to have a few friends from her own profession like. Help her remember the old days.

TED: She never stops.

BENSON: Only I knew they was here because they was seen in the Crown, apparently.

TED: In the snug?

BENSON: Only one of 'em asked for some peculiar drink and no one ever heard of it. Old Baldock says he don't believe there is such a drink and they just made it up like.

TED: Some cocktail, I expect.

BENSON: I dare say.

TED: Called a 'Gay Gordon' or something like that.
BENSON: Ah well, they'd be better off with a pint of Sam's cider.
Well, I hope your French stew goes down all right.
TED: So do I.
BENSON: Here we are then. Now, what are we going to give to
you, Captain Colditz? You don't make no trouble for
anyone, do you? *I* know what I got.

12. EXTERIOR. DAY. VILLAGE GREEN
TED, *his laden shopping-bag beside him, watches some boys playing
cricket. He looks around at the quiet scene. At some kids drinking
lemonade by the pavilion. The church clock chimes the hour. A few
dogs and their owners, shoppers, go by. A young girl on her horse.*

13. EXTERIOR. DAY VILLAGE GREEN
*Slowly, some of these people stop and turn to look down the road
leading into the village. A small boy runs towards them down the
street excitedly.*
BOY: (*Shouting*) They're here! They're coming! They're here.
They're on the way to the site. Some of them are there
already!
(*He dashes off to the boys on the green and they all double
back down the street. Everyone stops and waits.*)

14. EXTERIOR. DAY. VILLAGE STREET
TED *has now positioned himself with the other villagers so that he
can see the visitors.*

15. EXTERIOR. VILLAGE STREET
*Presently. A figure appears trooping steadily towards them. It is a
long-haired, bearded figure, carrying a rucksack, sleeping-bag, mugs
and guitar. The figure grows nearer. A second figure appears.
Someone shouts, 'Is that all!' Then, 'There's hundreds of 'em!'*

*The lone figure can be seen as only the leader of an endless army of
men, women and girls all dressed in the same convention, with
banners, odd guitars playing and so on. The usual circus as much as*

you like.

16. EXTERIOR. DAY. VILLAGE GREEN
Among the silent crowd a woman suddenly yells. 'My God! It's them! Thousands of them. It's them! It's all started!' She rushes away down the street.

17. EXTERIOR. DAY. ROAD INTO VILLAGE
Thousands of fans proceed in what seems to be an endless column. Line after line of them like a strange, advancing army with one purpose. Police are on the move with them and discreetly well in evidence. Wave after wave pass, as motor bikes and cars move up like supporting armour. On it goes towards Arkley.

18. EXTERIOR. DAY. VILLAGE STREET
The villagers and TED watch, mostly in silence.

19. EXTERIOR. DAY. AERIAL SHOT
Long stream of the pop procession, stretching across the soft countryside we saw at the beginning.

20. EXTERIOR. DAY. VILLAGE STREET
Presently. Three enormous Rolls-Royces sweep past the head of the advancing column and stop in front of the villagers. The front Rolls is a convertible and out of it steps LARRY BEST. Some of the others get out too, some of them offering flowers to the children and to the adults as well. LARRY approaches the crowd.
LARRY: Hi there, everybody!
CHILDREN: Hi!
LARRY: Come to give us a real welcome, eh?
    (*Children cheer. 'We want, etc.'*)
    That's the idea. We're all going to have a ball, you see, just everybody! and here it comes, kids, here it comes!

21. EXTERIOR. DAY. ROAD TO VILLAGE
The column looms larger.

22. EXTERIOR. DAY. VILLAGE STREET

LARRY *looks around at the startled villagers.*

LARRY: You've never seen anything like it! They've come from everywhere—Scotland, Wales, London, the States, Bosnia, Samarkand, Israel, Disneyland, you name it!

(*Some vans roll past and grind to a halt.*)

MAN: What's that?

LARRY: Television, squire, that's what it is, the tribunes of the people. There's dozens of them on the site already. There's enough cable in that twenty-acre field to lay across the Atlantic. All thanks to your kind farmer Duffard allowing us to use his field for this fabulous event.

VOICE: Yeh, and how much did you give him for it? Plenty!

LARRY: We made a more than generous offer and he was most delighted to accept.

VOICE: Greedy old bugger!

LARRY: It's a commercial game, man, and you're all in it whether you like it or not. I know some of you didn't like the idea of us coming here to your quaint little village—

VOICE: We don't now either! BOO! Do they know you're out, etc.

LARRY: We have created a new feature of the English countryside —the Arkley Pop Festival. Every year if we can arrange it.

VOICE: Over my dead body!

LARRY: No doubt it will, squire. No doubt it will. But we'll play you out real good.

(*Photographers have arrived and are photographing the bemused villagers.*)

This way, boys! I know, know. I say I *know*—let me have my rights, folks!

VOICE: Then let us have ours! Yes! Clear out!

LARRY: I say, I know some of you weren't so keen on the festival but we're here now, so cheer up and enjoy yourselves! You'll soon find it's real crazy!

VOICE: You're telling us!

LARRY: Now, come on, relax. You know me—Larry Best. And boy, I'm going to be good for you and better. The best manager and the best festival manager in the business. Why,

62

some of you won't be able to travel from one end of England to another without coming across one of my festivals. Let's *go*, man!

(LARRY *walks on, followed by group playing loudly, gets into his convertible Rolls and stands like some head of state waving to the crowds as his car glides in the van of the giant procession on towards the village hall.*)

23. EXTERIOR. DAY. VILLAGE STREET

TV REPORTER *is interviewing villagers.*

TV REPORTER: And what do *you* think about the Arkley festival, sir?

MAN: Ain't seen it yet.

TV REPORTER: But do you think it's a good thing?

MAN: Don't know do I.

VOICE: Rubbish! Shouldn't be allowed!
     (*Cheers.*)

TV REPORTER: And what about you, madam?

WOMAN: Oh, I quite like the noise. I quite like the music and that. Long as they clean up the mess afterwards.

TV REPORTER: Do you think there are adequate toilet facilities as Mr Best says?

MAN: Don't know yet, do we?

TV REPORTER: (*To* TED) And how do *you* feel about it, sir?

TED: Perhaps we could give them a rig out in the North Sea and pump the money in from there.

24. EXTERIOR. DAY. OUTSIDE VILLAGE HALL

DE WITT *and* LADY ARKLEY *glare from the steps at the army. The noise is quite deafening already.* LARRY *bows and waves to them.*

25. EXTERIOR. DAY. VILLAGE HALL

DE WITT: God knows what it will be like soon.

26. EXTERIOR. DAY. VILLAGE STREET

The tide moves on followed by the villagers growing rowdy and headed by the ringmaster, LARRY.

27. EXTERIOR. DAY. THE SITE

A huge field. In the middle is an enormous erection—for want of a better word—of scaffolding, platforms, loudspeakers, amplifiers, microphones and so on, all the quartermaster's small pop army of pioneers. Lavatories, stalls, kids, prams, cables, vans, bikes have already begun to work. A town is appearing and already the young people are streaming into the field, motor bikes snarl, trucks bounce across the earth, clothes come off and white bodies shine in the wan sunshine. Sounds and strange electronic noises come from the amplifiers and mikes. Coke bottles and transistors appear, children in prams. Etc.

28. INTERIOR. DAY. VILLAGE HALL

A small group of people, mostly middle-aged and elderly people. On the platform facing the hall is the 'Keep the Festival Out' Committee. In the chair is DE WITT. *The others are* LADY ARKLEY, *the* REV. DUCKWORTH, GROUP-CAPTAIN HEFFER, MISS BASTAPLE, MR DAVID BOLAS, SIR ARTHUR TRING, MRS STRINGER.

DE WITT *rises.*

DE WITT: Ladies and gentlemen.

    (*An early-warning amplifier sound shakes the building.*)

    Ladies and gentlemen. We are here, as you are well aware, to attend an extraordinary and final, I hope, meeting of the 'Stop the Festival' Committee.

HEFFER: Hear, hear.

MRS STRINGER: So do I.

DE WITT: Please. Have the minutes been distributed, Miss Bastaple?

MISS BASTAPLE: Yes, Mr De Witt.

DE WITT: Very well then. Let us proceed with the meeting before it's too late.

HEFFER: It's five past twelve. Not five minutes to.

MRS STRINGER: Oh, no, I can't agree. Supposing Churchill had said that at the fall of Poland?

HEFFER: France, madam.

MRS STRINGER: France then. We're all in Europe now, aren't we, France, Poland, Ireland's all the same. *He* wouldn't have

64

said it's five past twelve.

HEFFER: Ridiculous. This is *not* the Fall of France.

MRS STRINGER: (*Doggedly*) But it could be the fall of England and Parliament and even—the Queen.

MISS BASTAPLE: I agree and even Western civilisation as we know it today. And the whole Christian tradition, eh Vicar?

DUCKWORTH: Well, I wouldn't go so far . . .

LADY ARKLEY: Be quiet, Miss Bastaple. I thought you were taking the minutes?

BOLAS: Aren't we going to agree the minutes of the last meeting?

DE WITT: Is it necessary?

HEFFER: Of course not. This company—committee—is already in liquidation.

MRS STRINGER: Oh no it's not.

DE WITT: Very well then. Do we agree the minutes? Propose? (HEFFER's *hand*.) Second? (MRS STRINGER's *hand*.) Right. Now we can get on and get it over with. Incidentally, Sid is keeping the Dog and Rabbit open all day and this evening for emergency reasons until further notice—but *only* for members of this committee, this morning's meet and members of the Cowbridge Golf Club and Cowbridge and Brookfield Conservative Club and Brookfield District Rotarians. As we have three magistrates on the committee itself we had no trouble in issuing a special licence although Sergeant Brough seems to think the Chief Constable might take a slightly dim view. However, I'm sure we will have no difficulty when the time comes as Commander Harris is well known to Arkley and I know he loves it and has its future and its welfare close to his heart. I can't speak for the London police but, after all, they're not here to supervise licensing hours, but to enforce law and order.

MRS STRINGER: Hear, hear. You can trust the police anywhere in this country.

DE WITT: To continue, as you may know, this meeting was proposed by Mr Shilling. I must confess I was surprised, in the circumstances, that the committee agreed to his proposal.

C

However, some of them saw fit to give him a last chance and he is here to put some of his plans for your approval or disapproval. Before I call upon him, however, I propose to call up anyone either on the floor or on the platform to air any views they have upon the situation which I, personally, believe is now irredeemable and beyond recall.

VOICE: Rubbish! England looks to Arkley!

DE WITT: Would anyone care to start the ball rolling?

VOICE: Get out the bulldozers! Get the tractors!

DUCKWORTH: (*Rising*) Well, ladies and gentlemen, I'm afraid I have very little to add to what has been said many times in this hall during the past weeks. I fear that the Group-Captain is right when he says it is five past twelve.

MRS STRINGER: Oh, not *you*, Vicar!

DUCKWORTH: All we can do is offer up our private prayers—and I think it is important that we should do so today—as well as in church on Sunday. And if any of these young visitors to our little parish should decide to grace us with their presence at St Michael's we should do all we can to make them most welcome.

LADY ARKLEY: In our church? Never!

DUCKWORTH: Well, from what one reads in the newspapers, they do appear to be peaceable and loving and mostly law-abiding folk.

VOICE: What about Marie-Juna!

DUCKWORTH: Who?

VOICE: Pot!

DUCKWORTH: Oh, yes. Well, I believe the police are keeping a very strict eye on that situation. (*He sits down.*)

DE WITT: Anyone else?

MRS STRINGER: (*Rising*) Yes, I'd like to say a few words.

DE WITT: Very well. Try to make it short, Mrs Stringer.

MRS STRINGER: I just appeal to you all, at this final hour, for a little of the old Churchill spirit!

BOLAS: Cliché, cliché.

MRS STRINGER: I don't care. It's the truth. The eyes of the world are looking at *us*. It may sound funny but the future of us all could depend on this. On little old Arkley!

VOICE: Hear, hear!

MRS STRINGER: Today Arkley, tomorrow the World!

BOLAS: Oh dear, not this!

MRS STRINGER: When me and my husband first came to Arkley...

BOLAS: I'm supposed to write my monthly review of books for the BBC. How can I do it with all that racket going on?

MRS STRINGER: There you see. It's everyone! It's everyone suffers —not just ordinary people like me and my husband. When Mr Stringer and me sold our nice house in Hendon to come and live here—

BOLAS: Oh no.

MRS STRINGER: We thought we were going to really settle down to a nice, comfortable life—far from all the terrible things as they are in the world today. I was sorry to sell up my handbag shop. I used to meet some very interesting people. But then, this chain store made me this offer and I said 'What shall I do then?' And he said—my husband, you see —'You sell up and we'll get a nice little house in the country away from all the argie bargie while they still let you do it.' So we did. All our savings are here. And her ladyship has been so kind and the Vicar and Mr De Witt and the Group-Captain and—

MISS BASTAPLE: If Mr Duffard hadn't been so greedy and accepted all that money for his field—

BOLAS: Oh, not that again, Miss Bastaple! You must know farmers would sell their mothers and daughters for a barrel of cider.

LADY ARKLEY: Oh, *do* get on with it, George!

DE WITT: I *am* trying, Nora. Very well, if that is all—

BOLAS: It is.

HEFFER: Well, if *I'd* been offered it—

BOLAS: But you weren't.

LADY ARKLEY: Young Hornby-Smith, who made all that money in property, says he would have offered him that if he'd known he'd take it.

BOLAS: If our MP hadn't got his eye on the new young voters

67

and the new Cowbridge industrial estate—

MISS BASTAPLE: And fancy holding an event like this at *this* time of year! It'll soon be Christmas. I thought they did these things in the summer.

BOLAS: Mr Best says he's making it all year round the calendar. Now they come in furs and windproof tents. I'd have thought they were too soft, this lot.

HEFFER: Difficult to harden *them* up. Still more money in Best's pocket.

DE WITT: Order, order! Please! I call upon Mr Shilling.

TED: (*Rising*) Mr Chairman, ladies and gentlemen. I have a lot of misgivings about suggesting this last meeting for all kinds of complicated reasons. For one thing, I know I am not widely popular in Arkley like Mr Bolas.

BOLAS: Oh, do get on with it, Shilling.

TED: But then I work in a less popular field than he. Book criticism, for instance, seems quite popular, no doubt because it is a middle-brow kind of blood sport. My own work as a writer depends on myself only and that self, as my wife is constantly pointing out, is not very well liked. In fact, hardly at all.

BOLAS: Sounds like the opening chapter of one of your books.

DE WITT: Yes. Mr Shilling, Mr Bolas is a distinguished author himself, as well as a critic and broadcaster.

TED: (*Sneers, perhaps* one *too many at the Crown?*) Oh yes? 'Officer Material', a nosegay from the Royal Navy as it was. 'All the Nice Girls'—a novel and 'I laughed till I cried'— stalls-side reminiscences from nineteen-fifty to nineteen-seventy.

HEFFER: Steady on, Shilling.

TED: (*Secure in having got his jibe in*) Very well, this is what I propose. I'm always accused by people like yourselves of trying to push the clock forward. Well, I'm saying it may be five past twelve but we can still do it if we sink our differences. Maybe some good might come even from the combined effort if we fail—like the last war.

BOLAS: All we got out of that was Nationalisation, the Health

Service and Socialism.

TED: This is my plan. May I use that blackboard. We have to act at speed but I've made a few firm arrangements.

DE WITT: *Have* you!

TED: Perhaps the Group-Captain with his service experience could help me out with tactical and even strategic problems.

HEFFER: Glad to.

TED: And you too, Mr De Witt. And Lady Arkley's command in the Land Army. (*To* BOLAS.) The Pioneer Corps might be a helpful reference.

BOLAS: I was in the R.N.V.R. and you know it.

TED: Might help if the duck pond became strategic. What I am suggesting as an overall plan is like all great insights—like the Resurrection, Freud's theory of infant sexuality, penis envy or Parkinson's Law—shatteringly simple. Now—

29. INTERIOR. DAY. TED'S HOUSE. KITCHEN/DINING-ROOM
Very modern, comfortable and clearly efficient. Sitting at the large wooden dining-table are KIM, TED'S *wife, and her friend,* DEBBIE. KIM *is very smartly dressed, especially for the country and looks as if she had come straight off the London train. She is about forty but looks younger. She should do. Enough money has been spent on her looks.* DEBBIE *is a short, poor imitation of her friend.* KIM *is reading* Vogue *and* Harpers/Queen. DEBBIE *is reading a heavy book.*

KIM: (*Sighs*) Thank goodness you're staying with me for a bit longer, Debbie. I don't know how I could have stood it much longer.

DEBBIE: I knew it from your letters.

KIM: Well, I didn't hide much. Why should I? Anyone can see that Ted's not cut out for the country. Just because when he was a boy he thought he'd be a distinguished novelist, writing a thousand words before lunch, with a dim, plump wife and dozens of kids. That and taking the dog for a walk round the hedgerows before tea.

DEBBIE: Well, he's got the dog anyway.

KIM: Smelly old beast. He's just not got the style for it. People see through him. No background for it. Nobody likes him in the village except for old Baldock and some of that lot at the Crown, guzzling pints of beer and playing darts. He almost seems to like it. Except he's such an upstart. They see through him as well. They just let him buy them drinks. Now I *was* a country girl, I grew up with horses and point to points and all that. He thinks he can just poke fun at it and go along with it at the same time.

DEBBIE: Pathetic. *I* couldn't live here, I must say.

KIM: Well, neither can I. When that old crone Lady Arkley occasionally asks us over for sherry it's only because she's sorry for me. All he does is get drunk and insult the other guests. Last time he put a French letter in Mrs Hornby-Smith's chicken sandwich and she bit right into it. It wouldn't have been so bad but he'd put some yoghurt or something into it and her husband tried to take it out of her mouth and pulled out her top set.

DEBBIE: Schoolboy.

KIM: Well, we all seem to have that to put up with. Even you.

DEBBIE: Well, at least Jock is out of the house all day and doesn't get under my feet. Don't see him till the evening.

KIM: Exactly. That's the trouble with people like writers, they're in the *house* all day. Either that or reading in his room or out at the pub. Or, even worse, he's all over the kitchen. Not that I mind that much. It's something for him to play with. He seems to have lost all interest in work. Just because he thinks he's reached a watershed in his career as he calls it and is taking a break till the word strikes him again. Could be years at the rate *he's* going on.

DEBBIE: Seems in an alcoholic stupor most of the time.

KIM: He is. In spite of what he says.

DEBBIE: That's obvious to anyone.

KIM: He says the definition of an alcoholic is somebody who drinks more than you.

DEBBIE: Wasn't that Dylan Thomas?

KIM: Wouldn't be surprised. He ain't exactly original. He pinches half the things I say and puts them down, and then denies it. Says I don't understand the creative process or something.

70

Don't see anything creative about his process. Just drink and young dollies if he gets half a chance. We *never* go out— except to the cinema in Cowbridge or the little theatre in Brookfield. He won't join the tennis club for me there because he can't stand all those Young Conservatives. I said to him it's only because of your age, not your political convictions. As for London. We haven't been for weeks. He says it doesn't offer him anything any more. That it's too competitive and full of Yanks and Nips. The last time we went to the ballet he slept all the way through *Raymonda* and sent up everyone in the Crush Bar, including Gordon and Arthur. Fortunately Gordon wasn't dancing that night. He hates Gordon, says he's treacherous. Poor Gordon. When we went to Les A and Tramps—

DEBBIE: Divine!

KIM: He just pretended he couldn't hear because of the noise and kept singing 'It's My Mother's Birthday Today'! He didn't even give *my* mother anything today. Funny that.

DEBBIE: Isn't he making her a chocolate cake? I just *love* chocolate cake.

KIM: And what a performance *that* is! I don't know what he thinks he's proving. I thought he used to like her because she's got a bit of class as far as he's concerned and you know how class-conscious men from his background usually are.

DEBBIE: I know. It's so old fashioned.

KIM: He *is* old fashioned. Show him the newest fashion in anything, dress, make-up, hair, he just groans. God I'm so bored I could scream from the top of the church tower! I'm *glad* he's so mixed up about the blooming festival. He was too bloody timid when we came back from the South of France to find the squatters moved in. That's because he takes so long to make up his mind about anything. He thinks it more serious to bore everyone to distraction while he, God, makes up his famous creative mind.

DEBBIE: Stupid. Stupid and selfish.

KIM: If this is Getting Away from it All, I can't wait to get *back* to it all. That's why *I like* the pop festival. Bring some of it down *here*—please!

DEBBIE: Why don't you leave?

KIM: How can I? I haven't any money.

DEBBIE: What about your mother?

KIM: She's good for years yet. Besides she wouldn't give me anything while I'm still married to him. In case he got his hands on it.

DEBBIE: Why don't you marry someone else?

KIM: What, down here! Have you seen any of them! I say this looks interesting ('*Vogue*'.) I like that one. *And* that.

DEBBIE: You'd look marvellous in that.

KIM: I'll be lucky. Still, he might. Drop a few hints will you, darling? Then he might buy it out of desperation or boredom for Christmas or something and think he thought of it himself and what good taste he's got.

DEBBIE: Will do.

KIM: No, I can only wait now until he gets good and tired of all this capering about in this rural slum and we go back to good old-fashioned civilisation. . . .

30. INTERIOR. DAY. VILLAGE HALL

TED *is on his feet, pointing to a map of Arkley chalked in detail on the board.*

TED: That broadly is the plan. The strategic points are the church, which might even need defending—

DUCKWORTH: Oh, dear.

TED: The three hidden entrances to Twenty Acre Field here, here and here, the Gliding Club, out at Brookfield. They're already on standby for a phone call.

HEFFER: Really?

TED: The weather forecast is clear and sunny for the rest of the day. They will wait for a call from HQ here, and I suggest the Group-Captain to command the entire operation from here on. This job needs professionals.

HEFFER: Really—

TED: I leave it all entirely to you from here on. I've got lunch to get. The ground plan and the master strategy is there as I've described it to you. Mr Baldock will be waiting for the signal for his sheep. The same is true of Mr Duffard with his armoured column and his prize Friesians.

BOLAS: Old devil! Milking *both* sides!

TED: Except he insists on written confirmation of compensation for any damage to his equipment or his cattle.

DE WITT: He would—the scoundrel!

TED: Mr Baldock will do it for his services and his dog for a barrel of beer. I also had a word with the Joint-Master, who said they'd be ready on call at the Dog and Rabbit all day.

DE WITT: Did he indeed!

TED: He said he would only move in with cavalry if you approved the idea. I must say he was a bit dubious about the horses but he thought some of the young bloods would be pleased to round off a few hours' sport—especially if it's not been very good. They get very irritable if there's no good scent, as you know. He'll even have a cub ready.

DE WITT: You seem to have thought of everything.

TED: Dr Ford will be available and the District Nurse has come in on her bike to see her aunt. The Verger and bellringers are on standby all afternoon. I took the liberty, Vicar.

DUCKWORTH: Well!

TED: Well?

(*The Committee hesitates. They look at each other.*)

DE WITT: We don't want to break the law.

HEFFER: Why should we? We could say we're just having a bit of fun—like *they* are. *And* we'll be doing it on *our own ground*.

BOLAS: Crazy, if you ask me. Really amateurish.

TED: Isn't that what we English are supposed to be good at—especially in soldiering?

DE WITT: You're out of order, sir. Well, shall I put Mr Shilling's proposal to the meeting?

MRS STRINGER: Oh, yes.

HEFFER: Well—why not? Give it a sporting throw.

DE WITT: Very well then. If you think so. I don't think it's very wise.

MRS STRINGER: You would.

73

DE WITT: All those in favour of the motion.

(MRS STRINGER's *hand flies up, followed more slowly by* MISS BASTAPLE. *Then even more slowly by* HEFFER. *Then by* LADY ARKLEY.)

DE WITT: Those against.

(DUCKWORTH *raises his hand.*)

DUCKWORTH: I'm afraid I cannot support anything which could result in violence. I can't approve of the bellringers using their ancient skills in this militant way either. However, if the Verger has agreed, he's a very aggressive man and if he's had a few drinks at the Crown, as I'm sure he will have, it'll be difficult to stop him.

DE WITT: Anyone else?

(BOLAS *raises his hand.*)

MRS STRINGER: There! Three to two.

BOLAS: Mr Chairman?

DE WITT: Well, er, seeing that the Group-Captain and Lady Arkley have voted for it, I'll cast my vote with the majority.

BOLAS: Ridiculous!

DE WITT: I suggest, therefore, due to the pressure of time, we declare this meeting closed and the Committee discuss putting Mr Shilling's plans into action forthwith. Thank you, ladies and gentlemen, Mr Shilling. . . .

(*The villagers troop out followed by* TED.)

31. INTERIOR. DAY. VILLAGE HALL

HEFFER *on the platform at board.*

HEFFER: We'll establish communications here. Miss Bastaple will be in command. We'll liaise with all units by thirteen-thirty hours and, having checked tactics, aiming at seventeen hundred hours. Understand? Right—now then.

32. EXTERIOR. DAY. PATHWAY TO TED'S HOUSE

TED *is loaded down with his shopping and stares round at the piles of motor bikes.*

33. INTERIOR. DAY. TED'S HOUSE

TED *goes inside the door to see groups of young men and girls sprawled on the floor in various positions. A man approaches him.*

MAN: Hi, Ted. Shopping, man!

TED: Looks like it, doesn't it, me old Wandsworth guru.

MAN: Are you going to the big gig, man?

TED: I'll be there. Somewhere.

MAN: Great man, great.

34. INTERIOR. DAY. TED'S HOUSE. KITCHEN/DINING-ROOM

WINIFRED, KIM'S *mother, comes in. About eighty-five. Upright.*

KIM: Hello, Mama.

WINIFRED: Hullo, darling. Hullo, Debbie. How are you?

KIM: Bored.

WINIFRED: Oh, dear. I do wish you didn't get so easily bored.

KIM: So do I.

WINIFRED: There's always *something* to do.

KIM: Like what?

WINIFRED: There's always the Tennis Club. I thought you liked it before.

KIM: They're all ghastly. For once, Ted is quite right. Besides there's no one to give me a really decent game.

WINIFRED: Well, there's the garden.

KIM: And have it wrecked by those flowery yobbos? I *hate* gardening. And if you think I'm taking up bridge after a lifetime with *you*, you can think again.

WINIFRED: Oh dear, it does seem a shame. Ted seems to quite enjoy himself and keep himself occupied.

KIM: Keep himself *occupied*! What an odious expression—just being busy for the sake of being busy. (*To* DEBBIE.) I can't stand those people who say 'I'm *always* busy. Never get bored. Never get the time. Always something to do.'

WINIFRED: (*Not hearing this*) There's always something to do, darling. You were always busy when you were a little girl.

KIM: It's like married couples who say 'We never have a cross word.' Imagine what *hell* that must be!

WINIFRED: Why don't you go back to London if you find it so

difficult to live down here?

KIM: Because Ted refuses to budge, that's why!

WINIFRED: Oh, dear. I wish you could find some nice rich man who would look after you.

KIM: Find him!

WINIFRED: It doesn't seem to have worked out with you and Ted.

KIM: That's what I like about old people. Always first with the news.

WINIFRED: There must be somebody. I'm afraid you giving up your career was a terrible mistake.

KIM: You didn't say so at the time. You thought I was marrying a nice rich man to look after me and not depend on a precarious profession.

WINIFRED: Dame Ninette said you were the most original young dancer in the school.

KIM: Trust you, Mama, to tell me when it's too late! (*To* DEBBIE.) Do you know we haven't had it away since last August? Can you imagine that then?

DEBBIE: No.

WINIFRED: Had it what, darling?

KIM: Away, Mama. Off!

WINIFRED: Oh, I see. Well, as we all know, that's not everything.

KIM: With us it's *nothing*.

WINIFRED: There *are* other things.

KIM: Well, I haven't got any of those things either.

WINIFRED: When you're not *doing* anything, as you put it, you don't seem happy, and when you are, you don't seem any happier.

KIM: Oh, please, Mama! Not again!

DEBBIE: Is he really keen on that girl in the house there with that lot?

KIM: Shouldn't be surprised. He keeps going on about her big arse and those awful bristols as he calls them.

DEBBIE: Nauseating.

KIM: Good luck to them. As long as I get a good fat settlement and this house.

WINIFRED: But I thought you hated this house.

76

KIM: I do. But then I could sell it and get a nice flat in London with the money, and plenty left over.

WINIFRED: Well, you've always got Robert.

KIM: If you mean that shiftless son in their part of the house, you can forget all about him. He's like his father. Different style of generation, that's all. No ambition, hates work.

WINIFRED: Oh, dear, you do all seem to be in a pickle. Your father and I—

KIM: You and Daddy always had what you wanted. Houses, servants, capital, income, status, the lot.

WINIFRED: Well, of course, I suppose we *were* very lucky out there and especially at that time. Your father loved it out East. He didn't have to work too hard, and as you say, we had all we wanted. That is, before we lost it all with the war. Things were never the same again for all of us then. Kim had two Chinese amahs, you know.

KIM: Oh, here we go. I know it's your birthday, Mama, but do give us a rest.

WINIFRED: Sorry, darling.

KIM: Let's have a drink.

WINIFRED: Isn't it a bit early?

KIM: Not on your birthday it isn't. Come on, I'll open some of that champagne Ted brought in.

WINIFRED: I think I'll have a sherry just now.

KIM: Oh don't be such a drag, Mama.

35. INTERIOR. DAY. TED'S HOUSE

MAN: Oh, by the way, your toilet's had it. The seat's disappeared and the pan's packed up.

TED: Oh, Christ! (*He moves to the lavatory door.*)

MAN: I wouldn't go in if I were you. We'll get it cleaned up. Next week maybe. See you, man.

TED: Ta, ever so. Up the workers.

36. INTERIOR. DAY. KITCHEN/DINING-ROOM

TED *enters, struggling with his shopping, followed by Colditz. He looks at the three women.* KIM *goes back to* Vogue *and* DEBBIE *to her*

77

book. WINIFRED *smiles vaguely and takes out her library book from her bag.* TED *goes over to the kitchen area, takes off his coat, scarf and huge Augustus John-type hat and starts unpacking his shopping in silence with the dog beside him. After a while of this, he goes to the stove and peers into a huge saucepan and tastes the contents with a spoon.*

TED: Some bastard's pissed in my cassoulet! Which one was it? Own up! Debbie? Winifred? (*To* KIM.) You again! I know you pretend you don't like it but you always put enough of it away I notice. I was going to top that up for Winifred's birthday lunch.

KIM: Nonsense. Anyway, you know Mama can't eat anything but chicken.

TED: Well, she's a tough old pullet herself.

KIM: Ted!

TED: You know she's as deaf as a post. Like a nice, burning curry I suppose? Well, *that* lot's shot the cat with the airgun so you can have jellymeat whiskers vindaloo if you like. Give you the hot, steaming trots for a week that will.

KIM: Oh, get on with it if you must. You'll take hours as usual. I'm getting hungry already.

DEBBIE: So am I.

TED: Well, you do, don't you? What was it the doctor said about that hiatus hernia of yours?

DEBBIE: I must have something hot inside me in the morning.

TED: You'd be so lucky! Well, this'll be a hot one all right. (*He starts whistling and prepares his curry. To Colditz.*) What do you want, old son? Bit of something hot inside you? Even the dog's a pouf.

WINIFRED: What's that?

TED: A pouf, Winifred. Nancy boy in your day. Ginger, bent, gay. Blimey, if ever there was a misnomer, that's it. Gay. About as gay as a night in a Frinton whorehouse.

KIM: Oh, knock it off.

TED: Talking of that—your mates were seen in the Crown, of all places.

KIM: Who are you knocking now?

TED: Guess. Gordon and Arthur. They tripped in there looking for the American Bar I suppose. Thought it was the Gay Ploughboy.

KIM: Very droll. You're looking very pleased with yourself.

TED: Not yet I'm not but I will be. There you are, old son. (*Lays down the dog's dish.*)

KIM: Are you pissed again?

TED: No more than usual. Well man, I mean, Winifred, how's the old Blue Rinse Bridge Mafia going along then? Winning lots are you as ever?

WINIFRED: Just a couple of pounds.

TED: Good players are they then? At Lady Arkley's.

WINIFRED: Not very I'm afraid. She's quite good but the Admiral's asleep most of the time, Mr Bolas is a very poor player and this Miss Bastaple thought we were playing Auction last night. Nowadays—really!

TED: Poor old soul. Doesn't know her auction from her contract. Not up to Crockfords are we, down here, then, Winifred?

WINIFRED: I'm afraid not.

TED: Tough titty, old fruit.

KIM: He *is* drunk.

TED: Not at all. I just had a few pints with old Mr Baldock.

KIM: And Sam.

TED: Right and old Duffard the demon farmer. Oh, and a few others.

KIM: I'll bet. God, I hate pubs!

DEBBIE: And the men inside them.

TED: So how are you then, Debbie? Are you getting it? Lots of it with your Jock, I hope? You may not *want* it but it's the thought that counts isn't it?

KIM: That's *all* that counts with you!
    (*Pause. TED works.*)

WINIFRED: Oh, dear, you don't seem ever to be happy, any of you nowadays.

TED: *They're* happy in there. They've just busted the downstairs lavatory again. And they're happy because they know *I'm* paying for it. That's what *they* call socialism.

WINIFRED: Only, it *is* my birthday—

KIM: She's right. You might leave it alone just for once.

WINIFRED: Things used to be so different in my day.

TED: And so they were, Ma. You don't have to tell us. That's why we had Mr Macmillan's wind of change ten years ago thrust up our jacksies. You all had it sewn up pigging away in far flung imitation Weybridge, lording it over the lesser breeds without the law. Only you taught them a bit too much law and they used it against you eventually. Like our friends the hairy squatters. Good God, the B.O. in there!

WINIFRED: I'm sure we worked very hard. Kim's father certainly did. He did all he could for the natives.

TED: That's right. You brought them railways, hospitals, armies, the glories of the English language and the Bible and Book of Common Prayer.

WINIFRED: Yes. I suppose we did.

TED: And bridge parties, and booze, tennis tournaments, organised, respectable adultery, polo, pyjama parties.

WINIFRED: I don't think I ever went to one of those. Your father was very strict.

(*Pause.* TED *gets on with his cooking, whistling—or singing—loudly 'On the Road to Mandalay'. Presently he gazes across at the three women.*)

KIM: I wish you'd let that dog out if you're cooking. He smells.

TED: Colditz, you smell!

KIM: He's obviously dying to go out. He's only staying because of you.

TED: Come on, son. They don't want you.

(*Colditz follows* TED *to the door, which he opens.*)

There! Hauptsturmführer Kim says you must go out into the wider world alone.

KIM: Not in the hall. Outside I meant.

TED: There's so much piss out there from our peace-loving friends you need wellies up to your neck. (*He returns, humming 'Oh we don't want to lose you but we know you have to go'. Then, loudly, 'Your Queen and your country both need you so.'*) I wish she needed *me*. No gongs for you, old son.

80

Been married once too often for a start. (*Pause*) Well, how's the old culture up in the Big Smoke these days, Debbie? Keeping up with it still are you? Still reading the *New Statesman* and going to the Opera?

DEBBIE: (*Trying to force an effort at naturalness*) Well, no actually. We did go and see *Anastasia*. (*To* KIM.) Did you see Dowell in that?

KIM: Yes. He's superb.

TED: Ah. Pouf's football. All those fags up from the shires with their saddle-sore wives and eight children in the Crush Bar, hissing on about Dowell, and Rudi, and Merle and Beriosova, and Seymour and Sir Fred. All thinking it's A-R-T. Art! Instead of Victorian Court-bad-taste.

KIM: Don't let him.

TED: You see how *she* misses it? All those old mates of hers. All the tons of bouquets at the calls and the fans and the sheer *artistry* of it all?

KIM: Oh, you've started him.

DEBBIE (*Plugging on*) We went to a Mozart concert at the Festival Hall. Colin Davis.

TED: Good. Good. Reading some good books I see?

DEBBIE: I'm going through Turgenev again.

TED: Again! I'm always amazed at people who 'go through' books again. It sounds like going through childbirth again.

DEBBIE: It's great fun doing it for the second or third time. Like visiting an old friend over and over again. You both seem to change a little every time you visit them.

TED: Really? I know a girl who is *always* re-reading Proust. I couldn't get through it the first time.

DEBBIE: You should try.

TED: Why should I try?

DEBBIE: The result is just worth the effort that's all.

TED: Why don't you tell your friend there while she's deciding what's the newest shade in eye make-up. *She* hasn't read a book for years.

DEBBIE: I don't know but reading Turgenev makes me feel so Russian. I *am* part Russian, you know.

TED: I thought you were Bulgarian or something? Why don't you give Kim a book about making money—'The Shareholder's Book of Gifts' or an autobiography 'My Life with Ballet and Horses' or 'Starlight Nights' a Reminiscence of lost pre-war night clubs. The Golden Romance of the Four Hundred and the Café de Paris. That won't stop old Kim being bored. She wants to see it all there *now*. Before she gets too old and has to start going to the health farm six times a year instead of twice. Working away at the wrinkles, the stretch marks and cellulite before they stake their claim for good. It's a full-time job to work at and think about. Especially when you're so bored.

KIM: Listen, you. *I* am bored—with *myself*. Do you hear?

TED: You don't surprise me. Don't make a virtue out of it.

KIM: At least *I'm* not having a love affair with myself.

TED: Not an entirely happy one.

KIM: Oh, don't be so pompous. You sound like that awful David Bolas.

(*Pause.* TED *works in the kitchen then goes to the door.*)
Where are you going?

TED: To get the old lady's chocolate cake. I put it in their fridge.

KIM: What on earth for?

TED: Safer I thought than leaving it in here with Debbie. Hot inside her or not.

DEBBIE: I'm sorry—I just love chocolate cake.

TED: They've only got Coke and brown rice in there.

KIM: I'm getting hungry.

TED: You should have got up for breakfast.

KIM: Isn't there some smoked salmon?

DEBBIE: Oh, I adore smoked salmon. I was brought up on it. It was mother's milk to me.

TED: That must have been nice. Easy on your mother too.

DEBBIE: I'd like some of that wonderful Chinese seaweed now. I could live on it.

TED: You should.

37. INTERIOR. DAY. TED'S HOUSE

TED *closes the dining-room door. He goes into the sitting-room and looks around at the squatting and prone bodies.*

He goes over to a table, sits down, takes out a little piece of silver paper, cigarettes, cigarette machine and papers and rolls himself a joint. Some of the others are roused enough by this to stare. He lights up and inhales slowly and breathes out with apparent enjoyment. From the distance can be heard early sounds of the Festival. One of the young men strolls over to him, as he sits reading Melody Maker.

YOUNG MAN: Say, man, what you think you're doing?

TED: Smoking.

YOUNG MAN: Get that shit out of here. If the fuzz come up here again we'll get busted right out of here.

TED: Not unless *I* tell them.

(TED *looks at the* YOUNG MAN *and blows a lot more smoke into the room.*)

YOUNG MAN: You can smell that stuff a mile off. Hey, are you crazy!

(TED *moves out of the room. The* YOUNG MAN *starts trying to disperse the smell, waving a newspaper. Another one idly sprays an aerosol into the air. No one else stirs.*)

38. INTERIOR. DAY. LAVATORY

TED *opens the door and almost reels out. He puffs vigorously into it however. Then, he manages to reach the top of the cistern where he places a little white packet.*

39. INTERIOR. DAY. BEDROOM

TED *puffs away, placing the little white packets in hiding places all over the room.*

40. INTERIOR. DAY. BEDROOM NO 2

TED *repeats the same process, humming* 'Smoke gets in your Eyes'.

41. INTERIOR. DAY. BEDROOM NO 3

TED *repeats process, leisurely and carefully.*

42. INTERIOR. DAY. OTHER KITCHEN

TED *looks around at the turmoil, opens the fridge, which is filthy and takes out his chocolate cake, puffing smoke all the while.*

43. INTERIOR. DAY. TED'S STUDY

TED *sits at the desk, which is littered with cassettes and records. Puffing away and placing the packets in the drawer, he uses the telephone.*

TED: Arkley two-nought-seven? Sergeant Brough? Sorry to bother you today I didn't think I'd get you. I see. Well, when you've got time, I think you might like to come up here with a few of those chaps from Cowbridge. Yes. When you get a few moments. It shouldn't take long. This time you won't need the dogs. Right.

(TED *replaces phone and looks across the room to see* ROBERT, *his son, looking at him.*)

ROBERT: You bastard!

TED: Hullo, son. Have a joint?

ROBERT: You bastard!

TED: That's no way even for you to talk to your father.

ROBERT: You won't get away with it.

TED: Won't I? Sergeant Brough is a friend of mine. It's your word against mine. And you know how De Witt and Co are so hung up about pot. They are just not into your scene, man.

ROBERT: You can't do it.

TED: A father's evidence still counts a lot. Especially against his own son. You see, for once, today *I* am Establishment. Then I'll go back to the old way. Have you seen Slim?

ROBERT: No.

TED: Oh, I know, you're sore because I pinched your girl. See you in court—son. . . .

44. INTERIOR. DAY. KITCHEN/DINING-ROOM

KIM: If he goes on cooking all the morning, I'll go mad. I'll even end up playing bridge with Mama.

WINIFRED: There *aren't* any buses to Cowbridge today because of

84

the Festival.

KIM: Not Cowbridge, Mama. Why do you pretend you're not deaf and just *guess* all the time?

DEBBIE: They seem to be underway over there already.

KIM: It's hotting up a bit. Sounds fun. We must go over after lunch. (*To* WINIFRED.) I say, we must go over after lunch. If we ever get it.

(TED *enters carrying cake.*)

WINIFRED: I remember in Hong Kong they were always having festivals of one kind or another. And there were weddings and, of course, funerals. The Chinese have a great sense of fun and occasion. Kim's amah took her to hundreds of them. Oh, is that mine?

TED: That's right, Ma. If the Russians here don't get their hands on it. Just got to put a little message on it.

KIM: What are you putting on it?

TED: Winifred—eighteen-eighty-two to nineteen-seventy.

KIM: Don't be so stupid. It's like something written on a war memorial, for God's sake. People don't want to see their age on their birthday cake.

TED: *I* don't care.

KIM: *You* don't care about anything.

TED: No? Anyway. I suppose she *has* heard it now.

DEBBIE: Here, Kim. Write down what you want to put on it and I'll do it.

(KIM *thinks and writes on a piece of paper. While they are doing this,* TED *lights a cigarette, starts preparing his curry again. He starts humming, then whistling* 'Try a Little Tenderness'.)

TED: 'She may be weary
   Women do get weary
   Wearing the same shabby dress
   And when she's weary
   Try a little tenderness.'

KIM: Shut up.

TED: That's the real married-tart's song that is. Like it, Debbie?

(DEBBIE *is busily icing the cake and putting on its inscription.*

85

TED *continues to prepare curry and hum the same song.* KIM *goes on through* Vogue, *turning down pages.*)

45. EXTERIOR. DAY. HILLSIDE ABOVE ARKLEY
BALDOCK, *with his dogs, is whistling to them and seeing that the sheep are contained in something like a square. He stares down into the valley.*

46. EXTERIOR. DAY. THE VALLEY BELOW
The site is like a pinpointed black blot in the middle visible for miles around.

47. EXTERIOR. DAY. VILLAGE HIGH STREET
Streets mostly empty. Shops shuttered. LADY ARKLEY, *followed by obvious members of the W.I., marches to the hall. Martial music from here on.*

48. EXTERIOR. DAY. DUFFARD'S FARM
DUFFARD *is waving stick, lining up a formidable column of bulldozers and tractors while one of his farmhands drives the cows out into the the next field.*

49. INTERIOR. DAY. VILLAGE HALL
HEFFER *is directing operations with drawing-pins and tape on a board. Intense activity.* MISS BASTAPLE *on phone constantly.*

50. INTERIOR. DAY. CHURCH
DUCKWORTH *sprints around closing and bolting all doors. He looks at the bell-tower.*

51. INTERIOR. DAY. BELL-TOWER
The bell ringers are all lying on the floor, waiting, surrounded by beer bottles and sandwiches.

52. INTERIOR. DAY. BOLAS'S STUDY
BOLAS *gets up from his desk to close windows as noise from site gets closer.*

53. EXTERIOR. DAY. BROOKFIELD GLIDING CLUB
Men wait about in chairs, their 'crates' outside like engineless Spitfires.

54. INTERIOR. DAY. VILLAGE HALL
HEFFER *consults his watch and confers urgently with* DE WITT.

55. EXTERIOR. DAY. DOG AND RABBIT
Horses, dogs and hunt servants wait outside.

56. INTERIOR. DAY. DOG AND RABBIT
Hearty uproar inside the pub as members of the hunt celebrate.

57. EXTERIOR. DAY. HILLTOP
BALDOCK *whistles uncannily to his dogs. Wind blowing fiercely.*
BALDOCK: Don't fancy *their* chances.

58. INTERIOR. DAY. TED'S HOUSE
TED: Yes. Hong Kong must have been good in those days—for you. But where would you live now? If you could make a choice. France—frogs. America—no. Where?
KIM: Shut up. You're giving me a headache.
TED: It's going to get a lot noisier than this pretty soon.

59. EXTERIOR. DAY. DUFFARD'S FARM
The column of machines starts to move off, followed by the cows.

60. EXTERIOR. DAY. CHURCH
DUCKWORTH *hammers a sign upon the vestry door.* 'FIRST-AID STATION'.

61. INTERIOR. DAY. TED'S KITCHEN/DINING-ROOM
WINIFRED: It *is* nearer, isn't it? Oh, dear, I *hope* I shall get some sleep tonight.
(*Pause*)
KIM: Are you having an affair with that girl?
TED: Which girl?

KIM: You know who I mean. Robert's girl. . . .

TED: Yes.

KIM: What?

TED: Yes.

DEBBIE: Oh!

TED: Finished the cake?

(*Sings*)

'She may be weary

Women do get weary

Wearing the same shabby dress

And when she's weary

Try a little tenderness.'

DEBBIE: Do you *have* to?

TED: No. Do you? (*Hums*)

KIM: I knew it! Mama, I knew it! I only just said so to Debbie
before you came in.

TED: Then why are you surprised?

KIM: I'm not. I knew all along.

TED: You usually do. Pretty good at the old female precipitation
lark, aren't you? *I* was going to wait for the old lady's
birthday to be over.

WINIFRED: Now you could get him for adultery *and* non-
consummation!

TED: Non-what. Sorry, Ma. You only need the *one* shot. *You*
should know that. There's yours, standing in front of you.
(*Points to* KIM.) And don't think she'd divorce me when she
finds out how little she'd actually get. She'd rather live in
rich misery with me. But from now on, kiddo, there are
some things, if you want, you can pay for yourself. Like,
for instance:

KIM: I suppose you're going to spend it on your fat little dolly.

TED: Like, for instance: hairdressers, tennis club subscriptions,
massage lady from Brookfield at four quid a throw, Italian
lessons, face treatments. You can fork out a bit from that
capital the old man left you and you pretend doesn't exist,
I've had enough of you bumming off me and your poncy
friends, Gordon and Arthur and Debbie, the cultural turd

88

here. As for that superannuated, spoiled, old colonial ratbag there—

WINIFRED: It's all right, darling. His sort can't hurt me.

KIM: So, you're not going to marry your little mistress?

TED: Mistress! My God, what a white-centred bourgeois you are! Mistress! You actually make it sound cosy and quaint.

KIM: I expect she is. She's got the hips for it.

TED: And very nice too.

KIM: I suppose she rattles well, too, as you call it.

TED: (*Looming over her*) She bloody well does. Any old time of day and night. None of that Marriage Guidance guff about foreplay! Foreplay! That's what's disgusting about you frigid, nutcracker-legged man-haters—like you and Debbie here. (Christ, how did you get a name like that? Thought old film star names had gone out)—you're so genteel and dirty-minded. *She* doesn't just want it as a tribute. She likes it and lots of it, and if she doesn't get it, she doesn't make you feel like a washed-out rabbit!

KIM: Oh, I suppose she flatters you.

TED: Yes. And I flatter her. Which is pretty nice for both of us —if you're honest and she is, which is more than you've ever been with all your bored postures. She's my mistress and if you want to live with it in the manner to which you've become bizarrely accustomed, you can lump it with everything else; you cold-hearted, envious, uncharitable, venomous, vindictive, pig ignorant, humourless, boring bag of untender tripes. The Tender Tripes!

(WINIFRED *hits him on the face and nearly falls over.*)

O.K. Ladies. You've sounded the call. (*He picks up the cake from* DEBBIE. *To* WINIFRED:) *You're* too old. (*To* DEBBIE:) *You* like it! Have some Hot Mother's milk inside you. (*He smashes it carefully into her face.*)

62. INTERIOR. DAY. VILLAGE HALL

HEFFER *is looking at his watch, his arm upraised. Pause. He throws down his hand and* MISS BASTAPLE *picks up the phone and dials.*

63. EXTERIOR. DAY. HILLSIDE
BALDOCK *looks at his watch, whistles and calls to his dogs, and proceeds with his sheep down the hillside.*

64. EXTERIOR. DAY. ROAD TO SITE
DUFFARD'S *armoured column proceeds down the road. At the end is a barricade of police and vehicles. Suddenly, a farmhand opens a gate and the column turns off sharply into a field and disappears behind a clump of woodland.*

65. INTERIOR. DAY. CHURCH AND ALTAR
DUCKWORTH *is praying.*

66. INTERIOR. DAY. BELL-TOWER
The Verger finishes off a bottle of beer, and rolling up his sleeves, gives the nod to his colleagues.

67. EXTERIOR. DAY. CHURCH TOWER
The bells ring out.

68. EXTERIOR. DAY. HILLSIDE
The sound of bells in the valley mingling with the wind.

69. INTERIOR. DAY. BOLAS'S STUDY
BOLAS *puts his hands over his ears.*

70. EXTERIOR. DAY. BROOKFIELD GLIDING CLUB
Members wait, like Battle of Britain pilots. A phone rings. Suddenly a voice shouts and a man appears at the hut door. 'Scramble!' Siren!

71. EXTERIOR. DAY. DOG AND RABBIT
The Hunt waits in silence. Jangle of tack. The Joint Master. Waits, raises his arm and drops it. They move off to the sound of the horn.

72. INTERIOR. DAY. TED'S KITCHEN
KIM *is scraping the cake off* DEBBIE'S *face.*
KIM: He's *really* gone too far now. It's all out of control. I don't

know *what* happens now!

73. EXTERIOR. DAY. THE SITE
The by now cold fans are a bit restless, but still listening to the music. They can't do much else. LARRY *is cheering them on like a madman.*

74. EXTERIOR. DAY
TED AND SLIM *walk round the thousands of fans, holding hands.*
TED: Happy?
SLIM: You bet. You?
TED: Sure. I've done *one* right thing today. Maybe the other will work out too. We'll see. In time maybe.
   (*They walk on through the sea of men and girls, stewards, Hell's Angels, police, bikes, etc.* SLIM *looks up.*)
SLIM: What are those?

75. EXTERIOR. DAY. GLIDERS HOVERING AND WEAVING ABOVE

76. EXTERIOR. DAY. BELL-TOWER
The bell ringers swing vigorously on the ropes.

77. EXTERIOR. DAY. LOWER HILLSIDE
BALDOCK *and his herd are almost approaching the site.*

78. EXTERIOR. DAY. FIELD NEAR SITE
DUFFARD'*s armoured column advances.*

79. EXTERIOR. DAY
The Hunt moves into a trot, then the Joint Master raises his arm as the site moves into vision. Then he drops it with a fine cavalry flourish and the whole Hunt moves into a smart, almost military canter.

80. EXTERIOR. DAY
About a hundred yards from the frenzy of the site. A huntsman

*looks at his watch. Then opens a bag and holds a fox cub. He
releases it and it races off in the direction of the site. Then he
releases another and another—*

81. EXTERIOR. DAY. ROAD TO SITE
*As the Hunt moves on it faces a barricade of police. Suddenly the
Joint Master gives a signal and they too go through a side field and
some also jump over the hedge, making for the site in a different
place. The huntsman's horn sounds as they begin to break into a
gallop.*

82. EXTERIOR. DAY
*The next series of events will depend upon filming sequences and
resources. However, the true Battle of Arkley has clearly commenced.*
LARRY *is shouting and running around desperately; the fans look
astonished and unsure where to go. Fights start to break out and
grow in number. The police move in heavily. While this happens*
BALDOCK *has arrived with his sheep which charge fearfully into the
field, the police and fans trying to divert them vainly. Then:* FARMER
DUFFARD *and his farmhands urge on their front line of cows. Even
more chaos on Twenty Acre Field. Sheep and cattle mingle and
trample the crowd as people try to get out or fight the creatures out
of the way. After this, the next wave of Arkley Armoury moves in.*
DUFFARD's *farm machinery, bulldozers, etc.*

83. EXTERIOR. DAY. TED'S HOUSE
SGT BROUGH, *with constables and dogs, bursts into front door and
sniffs.*
SGT BROUGH: Right, lads! That's it!
(*They move in on the surprised, sleepy, remaining squatters.*)

84. EXTERIOR. DAY. THE SITE
*The fans charge through the battlefield, followed by the Hunt in full
cry. General panic. It starts to look really ugly—not Ealing comedy
at all. People are getting hurt and frightened on all sides.*

85. EXTERIOR. DAY
Those who can, look up into the sky.

86. EXTERIOR. DAY. SKY
The gliders are swooping, dropping all kinds of unwelcome things on to the field.

87. EXTERIOR. DAY. THE SITE
Struggles and mass panic as the different elements swirl about amongst each other. Horses, dogs, foxes, sheep, fox hounds, tractors, bulldozers, police vans, police dogs, loudspeakers, tents, toilets, stalls, makeshift huts, stands.

88. EXTERIOR. DAY. THE SITE
Vicious climax. It is indeed like a battlefield by now. People groaning and bloody, animals frightened, even the Hunt members look shaken and have taken some nasty falls, riderless horses, sheep, cows, all trampling in fright over bodies.

89. EXTERIOR. DAY. THE SITE
LARRY *is on the big rostrum as it starts to collapse. Still yelling, he goes down with it like a sea-captain on his bridge.*

90. EXTERIOR. DAY. THE SITE
DE WITT: (*Above the uproar*) Well—satisfied?
TED: No, but I never expected to be. (*He turns with* SLIM—*walks away.*)

91. EXTERIOR. DAY
Overhead shot of the site.